Billy Bunter Comes for Christmas

By the same author

Billy Bunter of Greyfriars School
Billy Bunter's Double
Billy Bunter Does His Best

Billy Bunter
Comes for Christmas

Frank Richards

*Edited by Kay King and
illustrated by Victor Ambrus*

A DRAGON BOOK

GRANADA
London Toronto Sydney New York

Published by Granada Publishing Limited in 1983

ISBN 0 583 30525 3

This edition first published in hardback by Quiller Press Ltd 1982
Copyright © text by Frank Richards and Kay King 1982
Copyright © illustrations Quiller Press Ltd 1982

Granada Publishing Limited
Frogmore, St Albans, Herts AL2 2NF
and
36 Golden Square, London W1R 4AH
515 Madison Avenue, New York, NY 10022, USA
117 York Street, Sydney, NSW 2000, Australia
60 International Blvd, Rexdale, Ontario, R9W 6J2, Canada
61 Beach Road, Auckland, New Zealand

Reproduced, printed and bound in Great Britain by
Hazell Watson & Viney Ltd,
Aylesbury, Bucks
Set in Times

Granada®
Granada Publishing®

Contents

CHAPTER 1

Snowy!

It was a cold and frosty morning in December, and the sky was overcast. An early fall of snow had sprinkled the grounds of Greyfriars School with white. There wasn't much of it, but there were drifts here and there among the elm trees, and little mounds had piled up along the edges of the grey stone walls. Groups of boys were making the most of it, and Harry Wharton and his friends were happily pelting each other with snowballs.

As Bob Cherry straightened up, his hands full of snow, he suddenly spotted William George Bunter, the fat Owl of the Remove, trundling into view. His short, fat legs, clad in tight checked trousers, were propelling him slowly across the quad towards the snow-splattered group.

Bob's eyes sparkled. 'Stop this one, Bunter!' he shouted, and hurled a snowball at him. Bob was a good shot, but it wouldn't have mattered if he'd been a bad one. Billy Bunter's roly-poly figure presented a very large target indeed.

As the Owl opened his mouth to speak, the snowball landed with a thump. It smashed against the tip of his fat little nose, and burst into feathery flakes so that his startled yell was muffled by the soft, wet snow that trickled into his mouth.

'Ugh! Oooooh!' spluttered Bunter.

There was a burst of laughter. 'Well stopped, Bunter!' roared Johnny Bull.

Bunter clawed the snow from his face, his small, round eyes glittering angrily from behind his large, round specs. Snowballing didn't appeal to him at the best of times. Come to that, exercise didn't appeal to him at all. As far as he was concerned, there was only one way to treat open spaces, and that was to ignore them, especially on a winter's day. His idea of a good time was to huddle in a comfortable armchair in the Rag, preferably with a handy bag of doughnuts by his side.

He was indignant at his reception. Clearly, those idiots didn't understand how difficult it had been to leave a roaring fire and go out into the cold, and he'd done it just for them. And look at his reward – a mouthful of beastly, wet snow!

'What did you do that for, Cherry?' he demanded. 'I came out specially to have a word—' He broke off, a look of alarm on his fat face. 'What are you doing, Wharton?'

'Cricket practice!' said Harry Wharton, briefly.

'But – but it's winter.'

'It's never too soon to start,' said the captain of the Remove, busily packing the soft snow into a hard ball. 'Catch, Bunter!'

'But – but – ouch!' Bunter caught it all right – right on the tip of his fat chin. 'Beast!'

'Butter fingers! Try again!' bellowed Johnny, hurling another.

'Our fat friend needs fielding practice,' observed Hurree Jamset Ram Singh, bowling accurately at Bunter's middle button.

'Keep your eye on the ball,' advised Frank Nugent, pitching a full toss.

'Ow! Crickey! Pack it up, you beasts! Oooh! Ouch!' Bunter became almost lively as he hopped and dodged, and twisted and turned, but he wasn't fast or nimble enough to avoid the hail of snowballs that landed on and around him.

'Garoo!' he wailed. 'Only came – ugh! Wanted a bit of a chinwag – oh, crumbs! Stoppit!' He almost fell over as a well-aimed snowball burst on the top of his head.

'Ha, ha, ha!' roared the Famous Five.

The Owl might be anxious to have a word with them, but they weren't at all keen to have one with him. They had a shrewd suspicion that his little chinwag had something to do with the Christmas holidays, and this was one way of avoiding it.

Then, quite unexpectedly, Billy Bunter, his little eyes gleaming with fury, stooped down and grabbed a fistful of snow. He rolled it into a ball, and flung it as hard as he could at Bob Cherry, but unlike the others, he was a rotten shot. It whizzed harmlessly over Bob's shoulder, and landed with a smart whack on the ear of a boy who was strolling past. The junior, taken by surprise, staggered, and then slipped on to the hard ground.

'Crickey!' muttered Bunter, and backed behind a large tree. He'd hit Vernon-Smith, and as he well knew, Smithy had a vile temper.

Hearing a thud, the Famous Five turned round, and laughed again as they saw the astonishment on Smithy's face.

Vernon-Smith clambered to his feet. 'You – you idiotic twits!' He eyed the snowballs in their hands. 'Which of you clowns clobbered me?'

Bob began to explain. 'Well, actually, Smithy, it was – it was—' but seeing a blob of snow sticking from the Bounder's ear, he started to laugh again. 'Ha, ha, ha! It – it – ha, ha, ha! Sorry, Smithy – but – it looks like an ear trumpet – ha, ha, ha!'

Vernon-Smith glowered. 'You great ape!' he hissed, and launched himself at Bob, and Bob, taken completely by surprise, went down. Smithy leaped on him, and ground his face into the snow before shovelling it down his neck.

'Get off!' mumbled Bob Cherry. He grabbed Smithy's leg, and tugged. 'It wasn't me—' but the rest of his words were smothered as Smithy savagely stuffed a fistful of snow into Bob's mouth.

Harry glanced at his friends. 'Come on. It's time we broke this up.'

After a bit of a struggle, they managed to drag the still furious Smithy away, but as Bob Cherry tried to get up, his feet slipped on the frozen ground.

'Help!' he shrieked, and grabbed at Johnny Bull for support.

Johnny, caught off balance, clutched at one end of Hurree Singh's scarf, and pulled. As the scarf tightened round Hurree's neck, he gurgled and desperately jerked it free, so that Johnny cannoned backwards into Frank, and Frank into Harry.

'Watch it!' shouted Harry, but he was too late. Quite suddenly, they all went down in a tangled heap. Yelling loudly, they flailed around in the snow.

The uproar attracted the attention of other juniors in the quad, and seeing a mass of bodies writhing around on the ground, they rushed up and piled into the fray. Snow flew

9

everywhere. No one really knew what was going on, or whether he was scrapping with friend or foe. That was unimportant. Being mixed up in it was what mattered.

Billy Bunter crept out from behind his hiding place, a delighted look on his face. 'Give it to them! That's right, Smithy! Go on, Johnny, keep on rubbing Cherry's nose in the snow. Good old Skinner! Shove some more down Wharton's neck!' He chuckled again. 'Rub it in old Singh's hair, Frank! Tee, hee, hee!'

He stood there, quivering with mirth as it went on, but eventually the juniors ran out of steam. As they began to sort themselves out, the fat Owl scuttled across the quad and made for the safety of the Rag.

Not that the fight had anything to do with him. He could hardly be blamed because Smithy had walked straight into his snowball, and it certainly wasn't his fault that Smithy had jumped to the conclusion that Bob had chucked it at him. Why, he'd have owned up if he'd been given the chance, he told himself virtuously. Nevertheless, he made up his mind to keep out of the Bounder's way for the time being, just in case any of those beasts sneaked on him.

As he sat by the fire in the common room, happily waiting for the joyful sound of the lunch bell, he made up his mind to give the Famous Five a wide berth too. It was true that he still hadn't managed to have his little talk with them, but perhaps it would be wiser to leave it until after lunch. He clasped his fat hands over his stomach, and sat back. Food, he reflected, always made fellows feel much more friendly.

CHAPTER 2

Just Like Bunter!

'Beasts!'

Lunch was over, but Billy Bunter looked positively disgruntled. It wasn't that he hadn't enjoyed it, because he had. The trouble was that he had spent so much time packing in as much as he could beneath his blazer, that he hadn't noticed everyone else racing out of the dinning room as soon as they were dismissed. He had completely forgotton that it was a half holiday and that most chaps would want to skate on the River Sark.

He mooched off to the common room, and stood there, his hands in his pockets, his eyes glued to the window, and then his gloomy face brightened as he saw Smithy walk briskly out of the gates and up the lane towards Courtfield. With the Bounder out of the way, he reckoned that it was safe enough for him to venture out, and so he made his way into the quad, and looked around.

His eyes gleamed as he spotted Lord Mauleverer ambling gently round and round on his own. 'I say, Mauly, old chap!' he called, but at the sound of his voice, Mauly put on an unexpected turn of speed, and disappeared from view. Bunter's face fell again. 'Beast!' he grunted.

He wandered towards the gates, a worried frown on his face. He had a problem, and he had to solve it. The problem was Christmas. The holidays were very close, but he hadn't any plans for it. He suspected that other chaps were getting together and making arrangements to spend Christmas together, but, much to his surprise, no one had yet sought him out and begged him to join in the festivities with the old folks at home.

And so he lolled against the wall, his fat brow wrinkled in thought. His efforts to chat up the Famous Five had come to nothing so far, and he rather thought that Mauly's rapid disappearance suggested that he wasn't too keen on a chat either.

He simply couldn't understand it. It wasn't as if he could be considered a bore. Everyone knew what good company he was – generous, thoughtful, entertaining and modest, but even so, it wasn't going to be easy to squeeze an invitation from either Wharton or Mauly.

If neither of them came up, what was he going to do? He ran his mind over the other chaps in the Remove. Some he dismissed immediately, feeling that they couldn't offer the degree of comfort that he expected. Others weren't in the running because they were joining parents abroad. He didn't even bother to consider Christmas at home. Bunter Villa with his parents, sister and brother certainly couldn't offer the kind of holiday that he was after.

He thought on. What about Smithy? Cardover House was grand enough. He could see it all – the laden table, glittering tree, splendid presents, and an army of servants, but somehow he couldn't quite picture himself in the middle of it. Sadly, he shook his head. Smithy would prove too hard a nut to crack. It would take a miracle to winkle an invitation out of him.

He shrugged heavily, and then shivered. It was getting chilly. He might just as well go indoors. It would be just as easy to think in the warmth of the common room.

He was just about to move when there was the sudden sound of pounding footsteps. Vernon-Smith sped round the corner and rushed through the gates, almost colliding with the Owl, and then skidded to a halt. As Bunter opened his mouth to protest, the Bounder thrust a packet into his hands. 'Quick!' he said, breathlessly.

'Eh? What?'

The Bounder looked towards the gates. 'Shove it in your pocket!' he panted.

'What?'

'Don't waste time, you fool! Get it out of sight!'

Bunter peered down. 'Crumbs! Cheesecake!' he gasped. He was holding a packet of cigarettes.

'Quick, fathead! Quelch will be here in a minute!'

Billy Bunter was no hero. He wasn't the type to risk his skin just to get someone else out of a hole, but since his form master wasn't even in sight, it seemed safe enough. As he slipped the cigarettes into his pocket, the Bounder nodded, and walked on into the quad. He was still breathing heavily, but he appeared perfectly composed.

Bunter stood where he was, his eyes fixed on the gates. 'Oh, lor'!' he mumbled, as the tall, angular figure of Mr Quelch appeared.

Although his form master wasn't actually running, he was taking long, rapid strides, covering the ground at a surprisingly fast pace. He swept past Bunter, hardly noticing him, his gimlet eyes fixed on the distant figure of Smithy.

'Vernon-Smith!' Quelch's deep voice carried right across the quad.

The Bounder looked round, as if surprised. 'Yes, sir?' he said, politely.

Quelch caught him up. 'Hand over those cigarettes!' he said, icily. 'Follow me to my study!'

'Cigarettes, Mr Quelch?' Smithy sounded astonished.

'I saw you with a packet of cigarettes when I passed you in the lane.'

'I think you must be mistaken, Mr Quelch,' said the Bounder, coolly.

'What?' Quelch was taken aback.

'I haven't any cigarettes, sir.'

Quelch gave him a long, hard look, his lips compressed. 'Follow me!' he said, after a moment or two. 'You will turn out your pockets when we reach my study.'

'Certainly, sir.'

Quelch frowned. He was certain that he had seen a packet of cigarettes in the boy's hand, but his confident air puzzled him. 'We shall see, Vernon-Smith!'

'Of course, sir.' As he followed his form master, Smithy winked at the small group of juniors who had witnessed the scene.

As they walked off, a broad grin spread across the fat Owl's face. Maybe the longed-for miracle had happened. Hadn't he just helped Smithy out, probably saving him from a swishing, and didn't one good turn deserve another? The very least that Smithy could do was to ask him to tea, and Smithy's teas weren't to be sneezed at. Furthermore, a friendly chat over tea might easily lead to a confidential talk about the hols.

Bunter wheeled his way indoors, plodded upstairs, and made his way to Smithy's study. He fished out the cigarettes and thoughtfully put them in the centre of the table where Smithy couldn't fail to notice them. Then he settled down in a comfortable armchair, folded his arms, and waited patiently for the Bounder, a smirk on his fat face.

He didn't have to wait for long. There was the sound of

13

rapid footsteps on the stairs, the door was flung open, and Smithy appeared. Billy Bunter, the self-satisfied grin still on his face, nodded towards the table.

'There you are, Smithy. Saved your bacon, didn't I, old man? It was pretty smart of me, catching on like that. I don't want to boast, but I really fooled that old trout Quelch. He swept through those gates like a bat out of hell. Didn't even give me a glance. Mind you, I'd made myself almost invisible. Hee, hee, hee! Lucky for you that I was around. I don't know what you'd——'

He stopped babbling, and stared at Smithy who was making frantic gestures. 'What's that for?' he demanded. 'I really pulled the wool – oh, crumbs!' He sat as if frozen, his mouth open, as he saw Quelch standing in the doorway.

Quelch pointed a long finger at the cigarettes, and the Bounder shot a look of loathing at Bunter.

'Vernon-Smith! Are those the cigarettes you were holding when I saw you?'

'Yes, sir!' There was no point in denying it.

'So you were lying when you said that you hadn't any cigarettes?'

Vernon-Smith hadn't actually lied. When Mr Quelch had asked him, he certainly didn't have any, but he knew better than to argue the point.

'You have behaved disgracefully. Had I not decided to search your study, you would have escaped punishment altogether.' Mr Quelch's voice became harsher. 'If you had owned up, you would have been punished, but because you have deceived me, your punishement will be far more severe.'

He looked at Bunter, who was still huddled in the armchair. 'Bunter!'

'What? Eh? Me? It – it wasn't me, sir. I – I wasn't there – at least, I was hardly there. That is, if I was, I didn't have a chance. He – he just shoved them at me. Don't like them. Not good for you. I – I wouldn't have touched them if I'd – I'd known they were cigarettes. Wouldn't. He – he just put them in my pocket when I wasn't looking. I——'

'That will do, Bunter!' snapped Quelch. 'You will write an essay on the dangers of smoking. I shall expect at least five hundred, well thought-out lines on the subject.'

He turned back to the Bounder. 'As for you, you wretched boy, you will return with me to my study!'

As Quelch and the Bounder left the study, Smithy swung round, and he shot a look of blistering hatred at the fat Owl.

'Oh, crumbs!' muttered Bunter, despondently. It was clear that Smithy was in for a swishing, and as soon as it was over, he'd be after the Bunter blood. He eased himself out of the chair. He'd have to keep out of the Bounder's way for as long as possible. As he trailed off, he shook his head sadly. The prospect of an invitation to Cardover House that had shone so brightly had suddenly been extinguished.

CHAPTER 3
And Just Like Bunter Again!

'Beasts!' said Billy Bunter.

After he had left the Bounder's study, he had made his way to Wharton's, hoping for tea, and he had bowled in, only to find that the room was empty.

His friendly smile was replaced by a look of indignation. Obviously, the Famous Five were still having a good time on the Sark. A fat lot they cared about hungry friends.

'Beasts!' he said again. For all they knew, he was starving to death. Greyfriars seemed to be full of selfish beasts these days. In fact, he seemed to be the only considerate chap around.

Crossly, he flung himself into an armchair, and then got up again. Restlessly, he crossed the room and poked his head round the door, listening hopefully for the cheerful voices of the Famous Five, but there was only silence.

He ambled to the window and squinted out. Although it was becoming dim, and he could see a number of fellows returning to school, there was no sign of them. He gave a snort. They were deliberately leaving it to the last possible moment before coming in.

'Selfish oiks!' he said, morosely. He'd had a rotten day. His failure to have a serious discussion about the hols still rankled, he'd got into Smithy's bad books, had collected five hundred lines, and what was more, he wanted his tea. If the Famous Five didn't come in soon, he'd be forced to join the rest of the mob in the dining room, and all he could hope for there was bread and butter, jam and buns. Why, a chap could fade away on a diet like that!

What was he to do? If he went down to the dining room, he'd risk missing tea in study no 1, but if he didn't he might risk missing tea altogether. It was a hideous choice. He turned the matter over. If he stayed there and then found that they hadn't anything to eat, he'd be scuppered. Well, there was one way of making sure. He gazed in the direction of the cupboard. If there was any grub around, that's where it would be. He'd be mad not to check up. If the cupboard was bare, then he'd go downstairs.

He threw open the cupboard door, and beamed.

'Tee, hee, hee!' His eyes glittered from behind his specs, for there, standing magnificently on a plate, was a very large fruit cake.

Bunter's podgy hands shot out, but then he paused. He seldom thought of the consequences where food was concerned, but this time he did. If he started on the cake and was found out, then bang went his chances of a friendly little pow-wow. On the other hand, he might not be asked to tea, and then he'd never have the chance of tasting it.

He gave an indignant grunt as he spotted crumbs on the plate and saw that a small chunk was missing. That settled it. They'd already had a go at it and hadn't even had the decency to offer him any. Without a doubt, they owed him some. Even so, he made up his mind not to be greedy. He'd just cut himself a sliver or two. They wouldn't notice that.

Carefully, he cut a wedge, and as he bit into it, a look of sheer delight spread across his face. It was just as delicious as it looked. He made up his mind to eat slowly so that he could enjoy every mouthful, but somehow, it disappeared in a flash.

Well, he thought, as he hacked off another piece, he'd have to do better this time, but in a miraculous way, it disappeared just as fast. Almost without thinking, he cut a third chunk, and shovelled it into his mouth. For a moment, he stopped and regarded the cake. It seemed to him that there was quite a lot left. He grabbed the knife, and dug in. A few minutes later, as he stretched out a fat paw, he was astounded to find that there was nothing left.

As he stood in front of the cupboard, he heard feet trampling upstairs, and the sound of cheerful voices. He blinked anxiously towards the study door, and then at the cupboard, and he moved quickly. Within seconds the cupboard was closed, and he was lolling back in the armchair.

The footsteps stopped outside the study. 'Right. That's settled,' said Harry. 'Tea in study no 1. We've got a cake. See what you can rustle up.'

'Okay,' said Bob. 'We might have some biscuits or something,' and he went off with Hurree Singh and Johnny Bull.

Frank Nugent pushed open the door. 'Oho!' he said, 'we've got an uninvited guest,' and Billy Bunter gave him an uneasy grin. 'Hope you made yourself at home,' Frank said, sarcastically.

'What do you want, fat man?' asked Harry.

'Er – well, I say!' began the Owl, nervously. 'I – I that is, I was just passing, and – and – I thought——'

Harry laughed. What with Christmas coming closer, the holidays in sight, and an exhilarating afternoon on the river, he was in a cheerful mood.

'All right, you fat freak,' he said. 'You can have tea with us. Frank, clear the table will you? Shove my books on the floor. I'll put the kettle on. Move your fat carcass, Bunter. Make yourself useful. Get the cake out of the cupboard.'

'What?' said Bunter, blankly.

'Get a move on,' said Frank, impatiently. 'Don't sit around like a stuffed dummy. The others will be here in a minute.'

'But – but——' The Owl was dismayed. 'I – I didn't come for tea, you know. Only dropped in. Thought we – we might have a chat about the hols and all that.'

'Oh, give it a miss, fatty! Heave yourself up, and get the cake out.'

17

Bunter's podgy hands shot out.

Bunter levered himself up. 'Can't stay,' he said, hastily. 'Really I can't. Got to – got see someone else. Just thought I'd give Harry the first chance of fixing up the hols with me. Been badgered by lots of other chaps but I told my father that I thought I'd spend Christmas with my best friends. Thought I'd write and say that I'm going to Wharton Lodge with you.' He blinked anxiously. 'How about that, Harry, old chap?'

Harry hesitated. He certainly didn't want the fat Owl for Christmas, but then, neither did anyone else. Having him around would be a bit of a pain, but he felt a twinge of sympathy for him. 'Twisting my arm, are you?' he said in a good-humoured way, and the Owl's eyes gleamed with eager anticipation. 'Well——'

He was interrupted by a howl of anguish from Frank. He was gazing at the plate. Their splendid cake had been reduced to a few miserable crumbs.

Bunter's face fell. His chance had gone. He took a nervous step towards the door. 'Have a word about it later on,' he mumbled.

'Where's the cake gone?' roared Frank.

Harry didn't bother to turn round. 'In the cupboard, of course.'

'Oh, yes?' Frank slammed the plate on the table, and advanced on Bunter. 'You fat villian! You greedy guzzler! You – you——'

'Me? Really, Frank——' Alarmed by the gleam in Frank's eye, Bunter sidled towards the door.

Frank lunged at him across the table. 'You pilfering poker! You——'

'If you've scoffed that cake, I'll——'

'No, I never!' hooted Bunter. 'Wouldn't. Didn't know——'

'Then where is it?' demanded Frank.

'It – it's a bit much picking on me,' gasped Bunter. 'I wouldn't touch anyone's cake. Not my way. Crikey! I never knew you'd got a fruit cake. I just called in for a chat about the hols——'

'Who had it then?' demanded Frank, edging round the table.

Bunter backed away. 'How should I know?' he howled.

'You must have eaten it, same as you did the bits that had gone. It wasn't there when I ate it, I tell you. No, not that. When I didn't eat it. Anyway, you hadn't left much. There were only a few rotten old bits – not that I saw it.'

'Scrag him!' shouted Frank.

'Let's boot him up and down the passage!'

'No! Stoppit! I bet you jolly well had it – whoops! Ouch! Yarooo!'

Yelling, he bolted outside. Frank and Harry only just got the tips of their shoes to his trousers, but howls of anguish floated up and down the passage. There was one spot of consolation for him, however. As he scooted downstairs, he was comforted by the thought that he was, at least, taking the cake with him.

CHAPTER 4

Nothing Doing!

'I say, Mauly!' A fat face peered round the study door.

'Don't!'

The fat Owl wrinkled his forehead. 'Eh? Don't what?'

'Don't say anything. Don't utter. Just shut the door and stay on the other side of it, there's a good fellow.'

Lord Mauleverer had been stretched out on his settee, relaxed and contented, his hands clasped behind his head, but that feeling of well-being evaporated as Bunter appeared.

'But – but Mauly, old man, I've only popped in for a minute.'

'The moment's gone,' said Mauly, 'so pop off again, there's a good chap.'

'But Mauly,' persisted Bunter. 'I came specially to have a little chat with you. I came up all those stairs and walked right along the passage. It's quite a way. Makes a chap hungry, all that exercise,' he added, hopefully.

As Mauly gave a loud sigh, Harry Wharton smiled. The two of them had been chattering away quite happily until the arrival of Bunter, but he was more forunate than Mauly. He was sitting in a high-backed chair which had its back to the door, so Bunter didn't know that he was there.

Billy Bunter stared unblinkingly at Mauly. He paused for a second, hoping to be invited in, but since no invitation was forthcoming, he entered just the same. 'I say,' he repeated.

'Oh, dear!' breathed Mauly. 'Must you?'

'Is something up?' asked Bunter, earnestly. 'You seemed as bright as a button when I looked in. Now you're properly down in the dumps. What's the matter, old man?'

'You!'

'Me?' Billy Bunter decided that he hadn't heard correctly.

'That's right, old thing. You've got it in one. Now be a good chap, and shut the door.'

'Righto!' Bunter obligingly shut the door but he remained inside the room. He had no intention of leaving until he'd had the little chinwag he'd been counting on.

Time was ticking by. The hols were looming. Soon everybody would be whooping it up for Christmas – everyone except for William George, it seemed. But still, the fat Owl wasn't the sort to give up hope. He was going to tackle Mauly, and he cast around in his mind for some way to bring up the subject.

'Seen anything of Wharton recently?' he asked, casually.

'Yaas!'

'Thought you might have done. I happened to hear him saying to Cherry that he was going to drop in on you this evening.'

Mauly yawned. 'Really?'

Bunter moved a little closer to him. 'It's just as well that he's been and gone.'

'But he——'

Bunter interrupted him. 'I don't suppose you wanted him hanging around here, cluttering up the place.'

'But he's——' began Mauly again.

'A bloated balloon!' The Owl waggled a fat finger at Mauly. 'There's no need to spell it out to me, old man. He's blown up, isn't he? Full of himself, but he's nothing but a windbag – selfish too. Not like some of us. Makes use of people too. I think it's amazing the way you put up with him, Mauly. You shouldn't. He'll only take advantage of you.'

Mauly smiled to himself, and Harry Wharton grinned as Bunter babbled on.

'Still, Mauly, I didn't come here to talk about Wharton. I came to ask your advice.'

'Oh?'

'Thought you were the best person to ask. The trouble is, I don't quite know what to do about Christmas. Wharton's the problem. I've stayed with his uncle before you know. I suppose he's got a nice enough little place in Sussex, but between you and me, I found it a bit poky. It's simply not what I'm used to. I wasn't particularly keen to go there, but Wharton put the pressure on, and I couldn't get out of it. Still, I don't think I could stand it again.'

'No?' Mauly lifted an eyebrow.

'No!' said Bunter, firmly. 'Of course, he's been on at me. Wants me to go again – thinks it raises the tone, I suppose, but I don't think I could put up with it again. It just isn't my style.'

'Really?' said Mauly, faintly.

Bunter shook his fat head. 'The truth is, I honestly think that you're about the only fellow in the form that I'd care to spend the hols with. What about it, Mauly? We've always been good friends. On the same wave length and all of that.'

'No!'

Billy Bunter took no notice. 'Mind you, old chap, it's nothing to do with your little place. Nothing to do with Mauleverer Towers at all. It's you. I've always liked you. I've stood up for you over and over again when other chaps have said that you're a yawning bore and a cracking ass.'

'Thanks,' murmured Mauly.

'Think nothing of it,' said the Owl, airily. 'And if anyone ever says that they heard me saying things like that about you, it was only a joke. Besides, I never did. In fact, I've often said that you're not the fool you look, and you're not as daft as you sound.'

As Mauly gaped at Bunter, Harry tried not to laugh aloud. The Owl was laying it on with a trowel, all right – or perhaps it would be more correct to say that he was laying it on all wrong.

Confident that he had laid the ground work, Bunter got down to brass tacks. 'Now, Mauly,' he said, briskly. 'What about it? I'm not actually booked up yet. I felt I'd like to give you first chance. I've already made up my mind to turn Wharton down. He won't like it. In fact, he'll probably turn quite nasty. Still, I've had more than enough of him. Anyway, the whole of his crew is going to be there, and they're not much more than a loud-mouthed pack of oiks. They can't help it, of course. It's the way they've been brought up.'

'Imagine!'

'Anyway, if I did go there, I'd have to put up with his uncle. It isn't his fault, but he's such a boring old fool——'

'Shut up, you ass!' said Mauly, quickly.

Billy Bunter didn't even hear him. 'And he's a stingy old beast. And there's his aunt – fuss, fuss, fuss. It's no good. I couldn't go there again. Wharton's all right in his way, but his relations are hardly out of the top drawer, are they?'

'You great, fat tick!' roared an angry voice.

Billy Bunter spun round. His eyes bulged as he saw Harry Wharton's angry face rising over the back of the armchair. He goggled. 'Oh, crikey!'

Harry leaped up, and Bunter took a step towards the door. 'Mind if I kick him out of your study, Mauly?'

'Not at all,' said Mauly, hospitably. 'Help yourself.' He looked up. 'There's no need to leave yet, Bunter,' he called, but he was too late. Bunter had fled.

Harry made for the passage. 'I'll chase that blithering idiot all over the school! I'll wear him down to a shadow! I'll wring his fat neck——'

'Now, now,' said Mauly. 'Sit down, Harry. There's no point in wasting energy. He'll be holed up by now. Whoever's lucky enough to have him will do the booting for you.'

CHAPTER 5
Cash Required

Mauly's guess was right. Bunter was holed up, but just for
once it was in his own study. Peter Todd and Tom Dutton
were doing their prep. Bunter, although sitting at the same
table with the same books open in front of him, wasn't doing
his. He was nibbling the end of his pen.

He was feeling gloomy. His chance of a happy landing for
the hols seemed as far away as ever. He pursed his lips as he
thought over recent events. He'd been unlucky. Why hadn't
that ass Mauly tipped him off? How was he supposed to know
that Wharton was in the study? It wasn't as if he'd hogged the
conversation. Mauly should have warned him. It wasn't fair.
Now he was back where he had started.

Where was he to go? Mauleverer Towers was out, Cardover
House was out, and he was pretty sure that there wasn't going
to be any invitation from Wharton now. The trouble with
Wharton was that he hadn't got a sense of humour. Anybody
else would have known that he had only been joking.

Dismally, he rocked backwards and forwards on his chair,
and then, quite suddenly, his brow cleared, and he began to
quiver with laughter. 'Hee, hee, hee! Hee, hee, hee!'

Peter Todd looked up. Tom Dutton didn't. He was
partially deaf, and that could be quite a blessing when the Owl
was around.

'Something funny about your maths?' asked Toddy.

'Maths?' Bunter was baffled. 'What maths?'

'Your maths prep, you clot!'

'Is that what we're supposed to be doing? No, it's not that. I
was just thinking.'

'You were doing what? Never!'

'Really, Toddy!' Bunter was quite hurt.

'Get on with it,' urged Toddy. 'You'll be in hot water

'Mind if I kick him out of your study, Mauly?'

tomorrow morning if you haven't finished it.'

'Blow prep!' said Bunter, loftily. 'The touble with you, Toddy, is that you can't see what really matters and what don't. Maths! Anyone with a bit of grey matter can do maths!'

'Then you've got a bit of a problem haven't you?'

'But I haven't!' said the Owl, triumphantly. 'That's where you're wrong. I haven't got a problem any more. I've solved it.' He chuckled again. 'I know you'd have liked to have asked me for Christmas, Toddy, and I'd have accepted if you weren't going abroad. Still, I've got it all worked out now. Wharton Lodge wasn't all that bad when I was there before. It was a bit cramped, I suppose, but you can't have everything, can you? I know that the Colonel's a bit of an old stick-in-the-mud, and Wharton and his mob get a bit oikish at times, but I've stuck it before, so I can stick it again.'

Toddy laughed. 'Why not put it round the other way, fatty. They've stuck it once. The question is, can they do it again?'

Bunter swept on. 'Wharton's been kicking up a bit of a fuss, Toddy,' he said, confidentially. 'We had a bit of a misunderstanding. Do you know, there's a nasty streak in him. Vindictive, that's what it is, but still, that's neither here nor there. If Colonel Wharton wants me to come for Christmas——'

Peter Todd looked surprised. 'Does he?'

'Does he what?'

'Want you for Christmas?'

'You never know,' said Billy Bunter, mysteriously. 'You never know,' and he gave another great, fat chuckle.

Peter stared. Something was stirring in that sluggish brain, but he hadn't the slightest idea of what it could be. He shrugged, and got down to his maths again.

'I say, Toddy!'

'Shut up! Get on with your maths!'

'Maths!' exclaimed the fat Owl, contemptuously. 'Blow maths, and blow prep! There are lots and lots of more important things in this world.'

Toddy went on working. 'Are there?'

Bunter threw down his pen. 'You should broaden your

horizon, Toddy.'

'If you don't get on with your work, your horizon will be limited to lines, lines, and yet more lines.'

'Don't you worry about me. I'll toss it off in a flash.' A cunning thought flashed into his mind. 'Why, I might even be able to give you a hand.'

'Really?'

'I wouldn't mind helping you out. I can check your work against mine when I've finished. I'll point out where you're wrong. All you've got to do is to leave your maths with me when prep's over, and I'll go over it while you go down to the Rag. How about that?'

Toddy laughed. 'Not likely. When Dutton and I go down to the common room, our work goes with us. We're not leaving it for you to copy, you lazy lump of lard!'

'There's no need to be insulting!' snapped Bunter, but then, remembering his scheme, he changed his tone. 'Of course you're right, Toddy. It's not a bad idea for you to get it wrong. You won't learn otherwise. That's what I was telling Quelch only the other day when we were having a little talk.'

'Oh, yes?' said Toddy, drily.

'Yes.' Bunter looked him straight in the eye. 'I told Quelch what a trier you were. To tell you the truth, I let him know that he just didn't know how to get the best out of you.'

'That was decent of you,' said Toddy, a touch of sarcasm in his voice.

'That's all right.' The Owl continued to stare at Toddy. 'I said a lot of other things about you. I told him what a generous nature you'd got.' He paused for a moment, and then said casually, 'By the way, Toddy, old man, can you lend me a quid?'

Toddy threw back his head and howled with laughter. 'That makes two of us. You're a trier too.'

'It'll only be for a day or two,' Bunter said, quickly. 'I'll pay you back out of my next postal order. I did tell you that there's one on the way, didn't I?'

'Oh, yes,' agreed Toddy. 'Frequently. Anyway, what do you want a quid for?'

'Well, you can't send telegrams without handing over cash,

can you?'

'A telegram?'

'Oh, well – yes – that is, no. Not a telegram – wasn't thinking of one. Didn't cross my mind, but they do cost money, don't they? Come on, Toddy. It's not much to ask of a pal. I must have a quid by tomorrow, and my postal order might not arrive by the first post——'

'Or the second,' grinned Toddy.

Bunter glared in disgust as Toddy went back to his work, and he turned his attention to Tom Dutton, who was still slogging away. He leaned across the table, and nudged him. 'Tom, old chap——'

Tom looked up. 'What do you want?'

'I want to speak to you.'

'Shriek?' Tom repeated. 'Who's shrieking?'

'Not shriek, Dutton! Speak!'

'Sneak? Who's a sneak?' he demanded, hotly.

'I didn't say sneak!' howled Bunter. 'Speak, that's what I said. Speak!'

'Freak? That's just as bad.' Tom rose to his feet and loomed over Bunter. 'It's about time that I taught you a lesson.'

'I – I wasn't calling you names, Tom, old chap. I just wanted to know if you'd lend me a pound.'

Tom frowned at him. 'No!'

'But – but Tom, old man. I – I really need it,' Bunter said, pathetically.

'What? I've lent you money more than once, and you've never paid it back.'

'But I will this time. I – I'll pay it all back at some time, honestly, Tom, old man.'

'That'll be the day.' Tom went back to his work.

'Stingy beast!' Bunter knew when he was defeated. He got up and made for the door.

Peter Todd turned round. Prep had to be done in studies, and nobody was allowed to leave until the bell had gone. Quelch was often on the prowl, and anyone wandering about was liable to be nabbed by him.

'I wouldn't risk it if I were you,' he said.

He was wasting his breath. Billy Bunter was single-minded.

Once he'd got an idea stuck in his fat head, nothing could dislodge it. It was the only thing that mattered, and what mattered at that moment was a one pound note.

'Blow prep! I'm going to push off. I'm going to have a word with Mauly. I reckon he owes me a favour. He messed things up for me, so he can jolly well stump up.'

'Think of Quelch!'

'Huh!' Billy Bunter flung open the study door. 'Pooh to Quelch, pooh to prep. You don't think I'm scared of that old misery, do you?'

He bowled round the corner, and walked straight into Mr Quelch. 'Oh!' he squawked.

'Bunter!'

'Oh, crikey!' Bunter went pale.

'Bunter!' repeated Quelch.

'Humbugs!' quavered the Owl.

'What was that you said as you left your study?'

'Oh, nothing, sir. I – I didn't say nothing, sir!' gabbled Bunter.

'I am well aware of the fact that you did not say nothing, Bunter. In fact, we might put it another way and say that you did say something.'

'It – it wasn't me,' said Bunter, hastily. 'I – I heard someone say that you were a misery, but – but it wasn't me. Came from miles and miles away. I was just going to find out who said it – wanted to give him a piece of my mind.'

'And what was that about humbugs?'

'It – it was just a way of speaking, Mr Quelch. I didn't mean that you were a humbug, sir, and even if I did, I wouldn't say so, not with you around.'

His form master looked thoughtfully at him. 'I am sometimes drawn to the conclusion that you are mad rather than bad, Bunter.'

'Yes, sir,' said the Owl, eagerly. 'That's me – mad, not bad.'

'And have you written that essay on the evils of smoking?'

'Oh, well, sir, I've – I've not exactly written it,' stammered Bunter, 'but I've – er – well, I've been thinking——'

Mr Quelch gave him a severe look. 'I see. You have not done it. Furthermore, although it is strictly against the rules,

29

you have left your study during prep. You will come to my room, Bunter!'

'Oh, lor'!' Dismally, the Owl trailed after his form master.

It wasn't long before he returned to study no 7, his fat hands gently massaging the seat of his trousers, and an expression of misery on his fat face. He spent the last few minutes of prep wriggling from side to side, the pressing problem of the pound note temporarily banished from his mind.

CHAPTER 6

Mysterious!

Although Bunter had forgotten about his need for a quid after his visit to Quelch the previous evening, it was uppermost in his mind when he awoke in the morning. A quid was what he wanted, and a quid was what he was going to get.

The first thing he did was to go to the letter rack, just in case his postal order had actually arrived. It wasn't that he really expected it, but there was always a faint hope that his father might have obliged for once – and it would have been for once. He hadn't, so although the Owl wasn't actually disappointed, he did heave a sigh. It just made his task that much harder.

The Owl was a ruthless borrower, and he set about his task with great determination, and by pleading with some, and refusing to take no for an answer from others, he acquired quite a little pile of coins.

And that was why when, after lunch, the Famous Five drifted into the quad, they came across an unexpected sight. There, leaning up against a tree, was Billy Bunter. In his grubby palm were the coins, and he was gazing at them.

It seemed a bit odd. No one could call Bunter a miser. Whatever he had, he spent, and he spent it eagerly, turning hard cash into cream buns, chocolate rolls, toffees and jam tarts as if he was a millionaire who had no need to worry about where the next meringue was coming from. But now, instead of spending, he was counting.

'Let's see,' he muttered. 'Here's ten pence, and here's another, and there's seven pence in my pocket. That makes twenty-nine. Twenty-nine, and these two halves, and those three from Squiff come to thirty-four. Thirty-four and five make forty – no, no. That's wrong. Forty-one, that's what it is. Add on this fifty, and I've got eighty-two all together.' He shoved the coins into one pocket, and dug a fat paw into another. 'Where's that other five pence got to?' He dug even deeper, and then brought out several more coins in his fist. He examined them carefully. 'Seven, eight, nine–eighty and nine make eighty-nine.' He frowned. 'Oh, crumbs! It'll take another thirteen to make a pound.'

There was a burst of laughter from the Famous Five, and he looked up, annoyed. 'What are you lot hooting for?' he demanded. 'Clear off! I've got work to do.'

He pulled out his accumulated wealth, and began mumbling again. 'Right. Fifty. Fifty and two tens makes sixty – no, no, that's not it.' He counted carefully on his fat fingers. 'Fifty, sixty, seventy. Good. Add on seven twos – that's eighteen, ain't it. Add eleven ones. That's – that's twenty-seven. Twenty-seven and seventy make ninety-five. Ninety-five and two halves brings it up to ninety-eight. Oh, coconut crunch! It still isn't a quid!'

'What did you say it came to?' asked Bob.

'What?' Bunter thought. 'Ninety-nine,' he said.

'And what did it come to the time before?'

Bunter looked doubtful. 'I'm pretty sure it was a pound and seven pence.'

'I'd stick to that,' advised Johnny. 'It sounds like the best bet to me,' and there was another burst of laughter.

'Don't be an ass, Bull!' said Bunter, sternly. 'This is important. It's – it's a matter of life and death. I've got to make it up to a quid.' He turned to Harry Wharton. 'What's seven twos, old chap?' he asked.

'Fourteen.'

'Are you sure? I thought it was eighteen.' He frowned

31

again, and they laughed. 'If you can't be serious, you can go away.'

Instead of moving off, the Famous Five looked on curiously as the Owl got down to his task.

'Now, what was I saying? Oh, yes. Seven twos are fourteen.' He looked scornfully at Wharton. 'Honestly, fancy thinking they were eighteen. I don't know why you're form captain when you don't even know a simple thing like that. Where had I got to?' He took a deep breath. 'Fourteen and eleven come to twenty-four——' He broke off and gave Frank Nugent a severe look. 'What are you sniggering for?'

'Sorry,' said Frank, humbly.

The Owl continued to clink his coins, each time getting a different answer, until Hurree Singh could bear it no longer.

'My dear fellow,' he said. 'You have ninety-eight pence.'

'Ninety-eight!' Bunter was dismayed. 'Oh, lor'! That's not a pound, is it?'

'No. You need two more.'

'Two? Are you sure?' Bunter fumbled in his pockets. He pulled out an old acid drop, looked at it with interest, shoved it into his mouth, and then examined the rest of the contents of his pockets. Suddenly, his face brightened, and he pulled out a coin. 'I've done it!' he exclaimed, triumphantly. 'A quid! A pound! One whole smacker! Dunno how much it'll be, but I bet it's something like that. Anyway, that's what I set my sights on, and that's what I've got. I wasn't going to Courtfield without it. It could have been a waste of time.'

'Courtfield!' said Bob. 'Why stagger all that way? You can blow it all on a beanfeast in the tuckshop here.'

'Tuck!' sniffed Bunter, disdainfully. 'Tuck! Some chaps think of nothing but their stomachs. Glad I'm not like that – not like some I could name. Anyway, this will do the trick.'

'What trick?' asked Bob.

'Oh, nothing,' replied Bunter, hastily. He slipped the coins into his pocket. 'By the way, you chaps, could you lend me——?'

'Time we got moving,' said Bob. 'There's still plenty of snow about, and I spy with my little eye a chap by the name of Coker. What about a spot of target practice?'

32

'Good idea,' said Johnny, enthusiastically.

'But I'm still talking!' hooted Bunter. 'You can't just go away when I'm talking to you.'

'Can't we?' said Bob, walking off.

'Listen!' said the Owl, desperately. 'I've only got this quid, and I've got to catch the bus to Courtfield. I need the fare.'

'What's wrong with your legs?'

Bunter stared down at them. 'Nothing. Why?'

'That's good. Use them.'

'But I can't trudge all that way through the snow – wouldn't get back for class, and that beast Quelch still wants that rotten old essay. He'll be down on me like a ton of bricks if I'm late. Come on – after all, we are pals,' and he stuck out his palm.

Frank inspected it. 'Needs washing. Try soap and water. It usually works.'

'Beast!'

Hurree Singh touched Bunter's finger tips, and stared thoughtfully at his palm. 'Ah, my friend. I see many things in your hand.'

The Owl looked impressed. 'Can you tell fortunes?' he asked eagerly.

Hurree nodded. 'I – I – yes, there is no doubt about it. It is very clear.'

'What is?'

'You will soon go on a long journey——'

'Really?' Bunter's eyes shone. Could it be to Wharton Lodge?

'Yes – you are going on a long journey——' Hurree Singh hesitated, and Bunter wriggled with excitement. 'To Court-field!'

Billy Bunter snatched his hand away. 'Beast! That's not funny!' he said, indignantly.

'But wait, my dear Bunter.' Hurree picked up his hand again. 'I also see something else. I see prosperity,' and he slipped a coin into Bunter's palm.

'That was jolly decent of you,' Harry said, as Hurree joined them.

'It was worth it. Now that we have disposed of the unlovely

33

Bunter, we can concentrate on more amusing things – baiting Coker, for instance.'

'I'll pay you back, Singh!' Bunter called after him. 'I'll pay you back just as soon as I get my postal order.'

'He'll get his postal order when you get your old age pension,' grinned Bob.

CHAPTER 7

Startling!

'Wharton here?' asked Vernon-Smith, as he walked into the Rag.

Harry, in a huddle with his friends, looked up. 'I'm over here, Smithy.'

The Bounder waved a newspaper at him. 'I thought you might like to have a look at this,' he said, and tossed it over. 'I've marked the bit I thought you'd be interested in.'

Harry picked the newspaper up, a puzzled look on his face. 'What? In this?' Newspapers didn't come very high on his reading list. In fact, Smithy was probably the only member of the Remove who ever bought one, and that was only because he was interested in the racing results.

'It caught my eye when I was flipping through it,' explained Smithy.

'What did?'

'The bit about your uncle. It must be him. It said Colonel Wharton of Wharton Lodge, and there can't be two of them about,' and Smithy sauntered off again.

Harry turned over the pages, and then stopped. 'Here it is,' he said, running his eyes down a short paragraph. 'Oh!' he said, and his face fell. 'Oh, that's tough! What bad luck!'

'What's up?' asked Bob.

'Gosh! I can hardly believe it! My uncle's house has been broken into.'

'Has he lost anything?'

'Yes. A picture.'

'Only a picture,' said Johnny. 'That's all right then.'

'What do you mean, you idiot? It wasn't just any old picture. It was his Tintoretto. You've seen it heaps of times. It was in the library.'

Johnny looked blank. 'A Tintorwhatto?'

'You ignorant clown, Johnny!' said Frank. 'Tintoretto was a great artist. His pictures are worth real money.'

'Hundreds?' asked Bob.

'Thousands – lots and lots of thousands,' replied Frank.

'That's right,' agreed Harry. 'A fantastic amount.'

'Phew!' said Johnny, impressed. 'Fancy having something worth that much.'

'It's been in the family for donkey's years,' Harry explained. 'I mean, Uncle James could hardly go out and buy another. He's not in that league. Mind you, it's not just the money. It's what it meant to him. He was absolutely potty about it. He used to go and look at it every day.'

'What does the newspaper say?' asked Hurree.

'Not much,' said Harry.

'Listen.' Bob Cherry picked it up, and began reading.

A burglary has been reported from Wimford in Surrey, at Wharton Lodge, the home of Colonel James Wharton. The alarm was given by Mr Wells, the butler. The burglar was chased, but he escaped through a window. It was later found that a valuable sixteenth century painting by Tintoretto had been cut from its frame. The police are investigating the theft.

'How rotten,' said Bob, sympathetically, and the rest of the Famous Five murmured in agreement. Because their parents were working or serving abroad, they had spent some of their holidays at Wharton Lodge, and both liked and admired Colonel Wharton and his wife.

'Fancy describing Tom Wells as a butler,' remarked Frank, and they smiled. Tom had been Colonel Wharton's batman, but he hardly saw himself as a servant.

'It makes it sound as if we've got an army of servants,' said Harry. 'In the old days, I suppose we would have done.

35

Nowadays Aunt Amy doesn't have half the help she needs.'

Johnny returned to the theft. 'Why did he bother to cut the picture from the frame?' he asked.

'You must remember it,' said Harry. 'It was huge. The burglar could hardly have tucked it underneath his arm. Mind you, the canvas on its own would have been pretty heavy. It wouldn't have been very easy to handle.'

As the worried look came back to his face, Bob gave him a hearty slap on the back. 'Cheer up, Harry. The police will catch the thief.'

'And he will not find it easy to dispose of such a valuable painting,' pointed out Hurree Singh.

'They'll get it back,' Frank said, reassuringly.

'I expect so,' said Harry, but he didn't sound convinced.

Suddenly the door of the common room opened, and a small boy put his head round the door. 'Here,' he said to Harry Wharton. 'Mr Quelch said to give it to you,' and he held out an envelope.

'Thanks.' Harry's face brightened. 'It's a telegram. I bet it's from Uncle James.'

'What would he send you one of those for?' asked Frank.

'Maybe it's to tell me that he's got the picture back.'

'But how would he know that you knew that it was pinched in the first place? After all, you only found out by chance.'

'Oh, shut up, Frank.' Bob Cherry turned to Harry. 'What does it say?'

Eagerly, Harry ripped open the envelope, and read the message. He gazed, bewildered, at his friends, shook his head, and then read it all over again.

'Is it from your uncle?'

'Yes, but——'

'About the Tintor – whatever his name is?'

'No! I don't get it. It's——' Harry was lost for words. Passing the telegram over to Bob, he flopped into a chair.

'I say!' Bob read out the message. 'Happy to see your friends at Christmas. Hope Bunter is coming. Should miss him.' He looked up. 'It's signed Uncle James. Well, that takes the cake!' He passed the slip of paper on to Hurree. 'Isn't that odd? Not a word about the picture – just a friendly word or two about the hols.'

Frank planted himself on the arm of Harry's chair. 'He can't be all that upset about the Tintoretto, or he would have mentioned it.'

'But why bother to send it?' asked Bob. 'After all, he knows we're all coming.'

'With our friend Bunter?' asked Hurree Singh, quietly.

Bob snapped his fingers. 'Aha! That's it. Hurree's right. He wanted to make sure that Bunter was included.'

Frank shook his head. 'I honestly thought he'd had more than enough of that fat freak the last time. It just shows how wrong you can be.'

'I thought he'd had Bunter right up his eyebrows,' grunted Johnny.

'Perhaps he thought that Bunter would be stranded,' suggested Bob.

'Like a whale,' murmured Hurree.

'With nowhere to go,' said Bob. 'It's jolly decent of him, isn't it? Fancy even considering that guzzling grunter after the way he behaved last time.'

'Mm!' Harry was still frowning. 'But I'm still staggered that he didn't even mention the theft.'

Hurree Singh looked thoughtful. 'Could it be that the telegram was sent before it had taken place?'

'Maybe that's it.'

'It should have the time when it was sent stamped on it somewhere,' Frank said.

Harry shrugged. 'Well, it doesn't matter. If Uncle James wants Bunter for Christmas, I'll just have to ask him. Sorry about that. We'll have to put up with him.'

'Don't worry,' grunted Johnny. 'If he drives you round the bend, we'll sit on his fat head until he promises to change his rotten ways.'

'He'll promise, all right,' said Bob. 'And then he'll get in our hair again, and then we'll sit on his head again, and then——'

'Shut up, Bob! It won't be all that bad,' said Frank, catching sight of Harry's gloomy face.

'Don't you give Bunter another thought. He'll toe the line.

I'll see to that,' promised Johnny.

The clanging of the bell put an end to the discussion, and as they left the Rag for their form room, Harry stuffed the telegram into his blazer pocket. He was still bothered by it – not a word about the picture, but several about the Owl. It all seemed so odd.

He tried to concentrate on the afternoon's lessons, but it was no good, and so, at the end of school, he went up to Mr Quelch and told him what had happened.

'And so I wondered, Mr Quelch,' he said, 'if I might use your telephone to ring my uncle.'

'Of course, Wharton,' said Quelch. 'I hope that your uncle will be able to give you good news.'

As he made his way to Quelch's study, Harry hoped so too.

CHAPTER 8

Harry Wharton is Not Amused

Once he was in Quelch's study, Harry dialled the number of Wharton Lodge, and his uncle answered the phone almost immediately.

'Uncle James,' began Harry.

'Is that you, Harry? Where are you?'

'At Greyfriars. I say, I read about the theft of the Tintoretto. Is——?'

'Not to worry,' said Uncle James, briskly. 'I was going to drop you a line about it. It hadn't occurred to me that you might already know.'

'I read it in the newspaper. I feel awful about it. I know what it meant to you.'

'It was a blow, Harry. I can't pretend that it wasn't, but I dare say that the police will get it back.'

'Have they any idea of who might have done it?'

'Not at the moment.'

'What actually happened?'

Colonel Wharton gave a little cough. 'Wells heard something in the night. He got up, and alerted me. Said he thought

38

someone was in the library, so we went down. We'd just reached the foot of the stairs when the library door opened, and there was dark figure with a large bundle under his arm. There was a bit of a scuffle, and the thief managed to break away from us. He rushed up the stairs and made for the attic. By the time that I got there, he'd already barricaded the door with that old iron bedstead. We forced our way in, but he'd gone. He'd escaped through that little window.'

Harry gave a little whistle. 'Gosh! It's terribly small.'

'I know, but then, he was a smallish man. He must have been very athletic since he got away by shinning down the drainpipe.'

'Gosh!' said Harry again. 'That must have taken a bit of nerve. It must be well over forty feet to the ground.'

'Yes, astonishing,' agreed the Colonel. 'After all, he'd still got the canvas under his arm.'

'Maybe he threw it down.'

'No. Never. The picture's far too valuable to be treated like that, and even if he had, he'd have had some trouble in locating it afterwards. It was pretty dark that night. In fact, if he'd been down there groping around for it, I'd have nabbed him. I rushed down the stairs as soon as I realized what had happened, but I was too late. I did catch a glimpse of a figure going over the wall, but that was all.'

'Like a cat.'

Colonel Wharton gave a short bark of laughter. 'More like a rat. Although the light was dim in the hall, Wells and I got a good look at him. I'll recognize him if ever I see him again.'

'Were you and Tom all right?'

'Oh, yes. He was as quick and nimble as a monkey. Actually, I rather think that he was more frightened of us than we were of him.'

'And what about Aunt Amy?'

The Colonel chuckled. 'Slept all through it. In fact, she was a bit put out when she found out that she'd missed all the excitement. Now, don't worry, Harry. With any luck it'll be hanging in the library again by Christmas. I must say I'm looking forward to seeing you all.'

'Oh, I forgot.' Harry pulled the crumpled envelope from his

pocket. 'I'll have a word with Bunter now that I've got your telegram.'

'Bunter? What about him, and what's that about a telegram?'

'The one you sent. It came this afternoon.'

There was a snort from the Colonel. 'I haven't sent a telegram.'

'But – but I've got it in my hands. 'Have – have you forgotten——?'

'Why should I send you one?' demanded Colonel Wharton.

'We – I – er – I don't know. It was about the hols. I thought——'

'What are you talking about, Harry? I can only think that someone with more money than sense is playing such a stupid joke on you. Now, goodbye. If there's any more news, I shall get in touch with you.'

'Goodbye, Uncle James.'

Harry put down the receiver, and stood thinking. If the telegram hadn't come from his uncle, who had sent it? He took it across to the window, and held it up to the light. He could easily make out the pencilled scrawl which showed the post office it came from. Courtfield, it said, not Wimford.

Harry snapped his fingers. 'That's it!' he exclaimed. Who had been to Courtfield after lunch? Who had been scrounging money? Who cared if Bunter was asked to Wharton Lodge or not? Only one person fitted the bill, and that was William George Bunter himself!

Harry charged out of Quelch's study, and raced down the corridor and up the stairs towards Bunter's study. That booby had almost got away with it. Well, now he was going to pay the price for his enterprise.

At the same moment that Harry was clattering up the stairs, Bunter was trundling into study no 1. 'I say——' he began.

'Not you again,' groaned Frank.

'Where's Wharton?'

'In Quelch's room.'

'Is he coming up to tea?'

'I expect so.'

They all scowled at the Owl. It was going to be hard enough having to put up with him in the holidays without having him haunt the study now.

'I'll wait.' Bunter rolled in, and blinked around, giving an indignant snort as he realized that no one was going to offer him a chair. He snorted again. It was going to be a bit much having to spend Christmas with oafs like that. However, the thought of the holidays made him snigger to himself. He'd really fooled them. What a pity he couldn't tell them about it.

There was the sound of pounding footsteps, and through the half open door they saw Harry dashing past. There was a crash as a door was thrown open, and then they heard his voice.

'Isn't Bunter here?'

'No. He might have rolled along to Mauly,' said Peter Todd.

The footsteps pounded back, and they glimpsed Harry rushing off in the opposite direction. Bunter smirked. He knew why Wharton was careering about like that. He was eager to offer that invitation.

There were more crashes up and down the corridor, and then the footsteps approached study no 1 again, and Harry hurtled in. He stopped as he saw the fat Owl.

'So here you are,' he said.

'Just wanted to have a word with you, old man.'

'That's funny. I wanted to have one with you.'

Bunter's eyes twinkled. 'Something special, was it?'

'Something very special.'

'Oh?'

'I just wanted to say——' Harry paused.

'Yes?' Bunter could hardly wait for what Harry would say next.

'You're a fat, double-dyed villain!'

'Eh?' Bunter could hardly believe his ears.

'You're as crooked as a corkscrew! You're a lying toad! What's more, I'm going to burst you all over this study! I'm going to——'

'Oh, really, Wharton!' bleated Bunter. This wasn't what he'd been expecting.

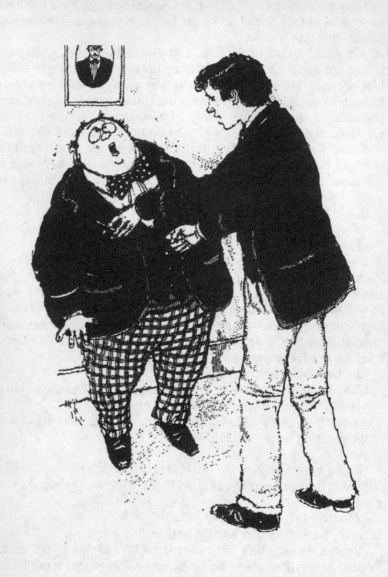

'You're as crooked as a corkscrew!'

The rest of the Famous Five looked astounded.

'What——?'

'Look at this! That gibbering idiot——' Harry fished out the telegram, and waved it in the air. 'Look at it, Bunter! Have you ever heard of people eating their words? Well, that's what you're going to do. You're going to eat your very own words. I'm going to shove this right down your fat throat!'

'But – but – I – I——'

'Oh!' said Bob. 'That's your——'

'That's right! That's my telegram. And who do you think sent it?'

'Could it possibly be our fat friend?'

'It is!' said Harry, grimly.

'Oh, crumbs! Oh, crikey!' quavered Bunter.

'You rotten rattlesnake!'

'I – I say. It wasn't me. Never went to Courtfield. I don't know nothing about a telegram.'

Johnny Bull shook his clenched fist underneath Bunter's fat little nose. 'Oh, yes, you did!'

'Never!' yapped the Owl. 'Never went near the post office, and I only wanted a – a stamp. Besides, I missed the bus – couldn't have gone. Didn't have the fare so——'

'You loathsome liar!'

Hurree Singh shook a finger at him. 'This is no joke, my friend. I rather think that you have committed a criminal offence.'

'Eh?' The Owl's face went white. 'Wh – what's that?'

'A crime,' Hurree repeated. He winked at the others. 'You have attached someone else's name to a telegram.'

'That's right,' agreed Bob. 'Quelch would take a very dim view of it.'

Bunter gave a yelp of alarm. 'Oh, crikey! Don't – don't tell Quelch. He – he might think I done it. Besides, I didn't. I – I didn't say Colonel Wharton, did I?'

'So what did you say?'

'Un – Uncle James, that's what I said. It – it could be anyone. There are lots of them, and——'

'Ha!' roared Bob, advancing on him. 'Now you've given yourself away.'

'Nun – nunno. I never. Don't know anything about it. Never went to the post office. Anyway, it was closed. All I did was buy a – a postcard when I wasn't there because the bus never came. It – it wasn't me. It – it must have been your uncle, Wharton.'

'Oh, no, it wasn't. I've just phoned him.'

'He – he forgot,' said Bunter, desperately. 'That's what he did. He forgot. He's a bit old and doddery, ain't he? It's softening of the brain, I——'

'I'll soften yours!' yelled Harry, lunging at him.

'Keep off!' howled Bunter. 'Only a joke. Leggo, you beast! Ouch! Keep your hands to yourself. Wasn't anywhere near——'

Five pairs of hands shot out and grabbed him, and rushed him into the passage. They raised him high in the air, and then they let go. There was a tremendous thud as he hit the ground.

'Oooooh! Ouch! Stoppit! Help! Ooooh!'

'And again,' said Harry, grimly, 'and then another, and one more for luck.'

'Ow! Wow! Aaaah! Yaroooo!'

As he landed on the ground for the last time, they marched inside the study, and slammed the door.

Billy Bunter lay there, groaning. He was even more disappointed than hurt. His happy haven for the hols had vanished, gone for ever, and there was nothing on the horizon to take its place. It looked as if it was going to be a bleak Christmas for William George Bunter.

CHAPTER 9

Breaking Up – and a Lift

'Bob, old chap.'

'Hallo, hallo, hallo! What do you want, Bunter?'

The Owl scurried up. 'I say, Bob, old man, what time are you leaving?'

Bob grinned. 'When we move off.'

'When's that?'

'When we leave.'

Bunter sniffed, as Bob strolled away. What an ass Cherry was! What he had wanted was information, and Cherry had deliberately kept it from him.

It was the last day of term, and most chaps had been busy all day. They had packed cases and trunks, shoved their books away in their studies, and got their sports gear together. Some had already left. The bus had been backwards and forwards to Courtfield station, and now it was standing outside the gates, waiting for another load of passengers.

Everyone was keen to get away – everyone except the Owl. He was hanging back. Although he was still not fixed up for the hols, he was determined not to go home for Christmas. He had watched the departure of Lord Mauleverer with a mournful air, and had sadly crossed Mauleverer Towers from his mental list of possible holiday homes.

But Bunter was an optimist. All was not lost. There was still Wharton Lodge. Of course, he was well aware that he had blotted his copy-book over the telegram, but Wharton was not the sort to hold grudges for long. As long as the Famous Five were around, there was hope, and so he watched them like a hawk. They would be going to the station by bus, and so would he. They would be sure to get into the same carriage, and so would he. He made up his mind that he would stick to them like glue and exert all his charm so that long before the journey was over, that invitation would be proffered and accepted.

He hurried after Bob. 'I suppose you'll be going on the next bus, Bob, old man,' he said, chummily.

'We might, old fishcake, but then again, we might not.'

'Stop messing about, Cherry!' snapped Bunter. 'Are you or aren't you?'

'Maybe, maybe not. I wouldn't like to say for sure. I wouldn't want to mislead you.'

'Beast!'

As Bob Cherry gave him a cheerful grin, the fattest member of the Remove rolled off, a frown on his fat brow. However, the frown was wiped away, and the Owl became wreathed in smiles as he ran into Johnny Bull.

'Hold on a minute, Johnny, old chap!' he squeaked.

Johnny gave him a cold stare. 'Want the tip of my shoe on the back of your trousers?'

'Eh? What? Of course I don't.'

'Then don't call me Johnny old chap.' Johnny strode off.

Bunter propped himself up against the wall, frowning once more but, as he spotted Hurree Singh hurrying into the quad, it was replaced by an ingratiating smile.

'I say, Hurree, it's jolly cold, ain't it?'

Hurree nodded. 'Yes. It's very cold indeed.'

'Must be tough on you, old man,' said Bunter, sympathetically. 'It's like an oven in your country, ain't it?'

'It can be very hot,' replied Hurree, briefly.

'Get frizzled up, don't you? Is that why you've all got black faces?'

Hurree shot him a look of contempt, and marched off, leaving Bunter puzzled. He didn't understand what had got into Hurree. He'd done his best to have an interesting conversation, and Hurree simply hadn't appreciated it.

However, he didn't waste any more time thinking about it. There was someone else to pounce on. Frank Nugent was coming out of the House. The Owl bustled up to him.

'So here you are, Frank, old fellow,' he said, breezily.

'That's right. Here I am.'

'Taking the bus to the station?'

'No.'

Billy Bunter's eyes popped. 'What? Not taking the bus?'

'No. The bus is taking me.'

Bunter's face went red. 'You silly ass!' he said, but then, remembering his mission in life, he gave a weak chuckle. 'No, no, didn't mean that. Jolly good joke. Tee, hee, hee!' He watched suspiciously as Frank bent down. 'What – what are you doing, old man?'

'Giving you something to remember me by,' and Frank hurled a snowball at him.

'Oooh! Beast!' Bunter wiped the snow from his face, and stared gloomily round the quad. Time was getting on, and still he hadn't got the information he wanted.

Just then, Harry emerged from the school, and walked briskly towards Frank. Bunter scuttled after him.

'I – I say, Harry!'

Harry halted. 'Buzz off, Bunter!'

'But – but——'

'Push off!'

Bunter looked hurt. 'I only wondered when you were leaving. After all, we go in the same direction. I thought we might as well catch the same train. Thought you'd enjoy travelling with me.'

'That's where you're wrong.'

'Oh, I say, Harry! I thought we were friends.'

Harry gave a short laugh. 'Then that's where you're wrong again. Anyway, you wouldn't really like being shut up with a loud-mouthed pack of oiks. It's not your style. Now clear off!'

'But – but I wouldn't mind,' said the Owl, earnestly. 'I – I know they really can't help it. It doesn't matter to me. I'm not a snob. I can get used to anything. Why, I wouldn't mind seeing you in the hols. Might brighten things up for you.'

'No. You wouldn't really enjoy seeing us at all.'

'But I would.'

'But you wouldn't, and I'll tell you why. If we catch a glimpse of your fat face, we're going to kick you from one end of the county to the other,' and Harry shook off Bunter's fat paw, and hurried on.

'Beast!'

However, in spite of his rebuffs, he hovered in the quad, alert for the first signs of their departure. They weren't getting away without him if he could help it.

His vigilance was rewarded at last. Laughing and chattering, the Famous Five clambered on to the bus as the driver switched on his engine. Bunter grabbed his bags which he had carefully left by the gates, and charged through a group of juniors who were still hanging about.

'Wait for me!' he yelled. A foot got in his way, and he went sprawling into the snow. 'Yaroooo!' he wailed.

The fellows in the bus pressed their faces to the window, and roared with laughter at his look of baffled fury. Bob Cherry gave Tom Redwing an appreciative grin, and Redwing,

47

whose foot had tripped Bunter up, grinned back.

'Ow, wow!' moaned Bunter, as the bus drove off. He sat up, spluttering.

'Goodbye, Bunter!'

'Cheerio, fat man!'

'Have a nice Christmas, Bunter!'

Bunter sat in the wet snow, dismayed. They'd gone. They'd escaped after all. Now what was he going to do? It was quite late in the afternoon, the light was beginning to fade, and there were very few chaps around.

Suddenly, he scrambled to his feet and trotted after a figure walking back into the quad. 'Smithy!' he called.

'Don't bother!'

'But I say, Smithy——'

Vernon-Smith turned round and gave the Owl an impatient stare. 'What do you want?'

Bunter's eyes were glued to Smithy's father's Rolls, gleaming grandly in the quad. It didn't seem very likely, but there was always a chance that the Bounder might give him a lift.

'Well, you see, Smithy,' he began. 'It's like this. I was going on the same train as Wharton and his crowd, but I – I missed the bus. I thought you might help me out, old man, and give me a lift——'

'What!' snapped the Bounder.

'Just – just as far as Wharton Lodge, Smithy.'

'Wharton Lodge?' Smithy raised his eyebrows in surprise.

'That's it. I know it would take you a bit out of your way, but it don't mean a thing, not with a car like that.'

'Oh, no,' said the Bounder, sarcastically. 'Only another fifty miles or so.'

'You see, I've got to get there somehow,' said Bunter, urgently.

'You could catch a train.'

'I – I know, but I'd rather get there before they do, now that I've missed the train. It – it would have been all right if I'd gone with them. Would have sorted things out with Wharton.'

'Oh?'

'We – we had a little misunderstanding – nothing much. I

48

can't understand how it happened. But if I got there first, and Colonel Wharton welcomed me as the advance guard, he'd think that Harry had asked me, and then I'd be all right.'

'What was this little misunderstanding?'

'Nothing, nothing at all,' said Bunter, airily. 'It was all about a telegram I hadn't sent. Wharton knew I'd told my father I was spending Christmas with him, but he got really shirty over the telegram. As if I'd call myself Uncle James. Wouldn't dream of it. And he was only joking when he said he'd boot me all over the county if he caught sight of me, so that's why I'd like to get there first. Can't boot a guest, can you? So that's why a lift –' His voice trailed away as Smithy gave him a long, hard look.

Smithy grinned to himself. He could see Bunter's game. He was going to con his way into Wharton Lodge. 'Righto,' he said. 'Get your bags, and hop in.'

Billy Bunter gleamed. He could hardly believe his luck. 'Oh, thanks, Smithy. Won't be a tick.'

He rushed across to the gates, seized his cases, and scuttled back. While Smithy was talking to the chauffeur, he hopped in, smirking.

At last, Smithy clambered in, and the car rolled off. As they went along, Smithy glanced from time to time at Bunter, a sardonic look on his face. The Owl neither knew nor cared what that look was for. He'd got his lift, and a very superior lift at that.

'Quite a nice little bus,' he said, chattily. 'Couldn't help noticing that it's last year's registration number. My father changes his car every year. He reckons that getting a new Rolls is an economy really.'

'Oh.'

There was a long period of silence until Bunter spoke again. 'Got any chocs, Smithy?'

'No.'

'Not even an acid drop?'

'No.'

'I say, Smithy. It was a bit late when we started. I'm getting a bit peckish, aren't you? What about stopping for a snack.'

'No.'

49

'Oh.' Bunter relapsed into silence.

A little later, quite unexpectedly, the Bounder fumbled in his pocket and brought out a slab of toffee. 'Look what I've found. You can have it.'

He unwrapped it, and passed it over, but somehow, he knocked the Owl's glasses off. 'Sorry,' he said, and picked them up. 'They've got a bit smeary. I'll clean them up for you in a minute.'

Bunter didn't care. He shoved the toffee into his mouth, and went on chewing rhythmically as the car rolled on. Suddenly, it stopped, and Bunter peered out. It was very dark by now.

'Here we are,' said the Bounder, breezily.

Bunter screwed up his eyes. 'Have we got to Wharton Lodge,' he asked, unable to see any lights.

'Yes, fathead. We're going to walk the rest of the way.'

'Walk?' said Bunter, blankly.

'That's right. I want to stretch my legs. Out!'

Reluctantly, the Owl climbed out. 'How far?'

'It's quite close.'

Bunter clung to Smithy's arm. 'I can't see where I'm going,' he complained. 'Where are my specs?' The Bounder handed them to him. 'Oh, I say, Smithy. What have you done? They're worse than ever. I can't see a thing.'

'You can clean them up when you get inside.'

The Owl blinked round. He could just make out the shape of the trees, the snow on their branches making them look positively ghostly in the dark. Suddenly there was a hard hand on his shoulder.

'Wh – what – ow!' he yelled, as he was pushed into a hedge.

There was the sound of running footsteps, the purr of an engine, and then the Rolls moved off, its tail lights disappearing in the distance.

'Smithy!' yelled Bunter. 'Smithy, you beast!'

He blundered around, wondering just where he was, and then he felt a wooden gate. Had Smithy dropped him at a side entrance to Wharton Lodge? He pulled out a grubby handkerchief, and tried to clean his glasses, and then turned

. . . he felt a wooden gate.

51

back to the gate. Something was written on it, and he traced the letters with a fat finger.

'Oh!' he gasped. It was Bunter Villa!

CHAPTER 10
A Talk on the Telephone

Bob Cherry stood by the window. 'It's fabulous!' he exclaimed, enthusiastically.

Bob was always inclined to be enthusiastic, but he wasn't exaggerating. It was fabulous. There had been a heavy fall of snow during the night and the grounds of Wharton Lodge were covered in dazzling white.

'It looks like a picture on a Christmas card,' said Hurree Singh, appreciatively.

Harry Wharton smiled. Life was marvellous. Here he was, home for the holidays, his friends by his side. The house was decorated with holly and ivy, and there was the wonderful smell of Christmas food coming from the kitchen. The only little bit of gloom on the horizon was the loss of the Tintoretto, but his uncle still sounded very optimistic about his chances of getting it back.

'I've had a word with Tom Wells,' Harry said. 'He said that the lake's frozen solid. What about going skating this morning?'

'Smashing!' said Bob, and then he laughed. 'Do you remember what happened the last time when you had that fat sausage staying? He did practically all of his skating sitting down.'

'That's right. He couldn't get up. We had to drag him off the lake in the end.'

'It was hard work,' said Johnny. 'He must have weighed as much as an elephant.'

'He still does,' Frank pointed out.

'Poor old Bunter,' said Hurree.

'Oh, yes?' said Johnny. 'He did his best to mess up our holiday, didn't he?'

'Jolly good thing he didn't get away with it,' remarked Bob. 'It would have ruined everything.'

'Let's forget him.'

'Out of sight is out of mind,' observed Hurree, but he was wrong. Billy Bunter was out of sight all right, but he wasn't going to be out of their minds for long.

Tom Wells appeared. 'There's a phone call for you,' he said to Harry.

'For me?'

'Yes, it's your friend Bunter.'

'He must have known we were talking about him,' said Bob.

Frank smiled at Harry. 'Maybe he's just rung up to say Happy Christmas.'

'And maybe not,' said Harry, as he went into the hall. As he picked up the receiver, he could hear the Owl squawking indignantly.

'Wharton! Lazy beast! What's keeping him? Oiks!' There was a short pause, and then he said. 'Hallo, hallo! Come on, Wharton, you beast! Wharton!'

'Hallo,' said Harry, trying not to laugh.

'Oh, is that you, Harry, old chap? I say, old man——'

'Make it short, fatty. I'm going out.'

'Oh, I say, that's not very friendly!' said Bunter, indignantly.

'That's right. I'm not feeling particularly friendly. Well, if that's all you——'

'No, it isn't, you beast! That is, I – I mean——'

'Well, what do you mean?'

'I got up early specially to wish you a happy Christmas——'

'Thanks. Same to you. Goodbye.'

'Hang on!' howled Bunter. 'I haven't finished yet. I say, seeing that we're such good friends, Harry, I was thinking of dropping in to see you.'

'Then think again,' said Harry, curtly.

'Mind you, it won't be all that easy. Invitations keep flooding in. You know how it is when you're as popular as I am.'

'Good. Accept them.'

'But I still might be able to fit you in, Harry. I hope you ain't still shirty about that telegram. It was only a little misunderstanding after all. Anyway, I never sent it, and it was just a little joke – hee, hee, hee! I'll tell you what. I could hop on a train. If I got a move on, I could arrive in time for lunch. How would you like that?'

'I wouldn't.'

'Oh!' Bunter sounded dismayed. 'But——'

'And a Merry Christmas to you, you soggy sardine, and the same goes for the rest of the oiks!'

Harry put down the receiver and joined the others who were standing outside in the porch, surveying the snowy scene. The phone rang again. Harry made a face at them, and went in and picked it up again.

'Is that you, old fellow?' As he had expected, it was the fat Owl again.

'Yes, it is, you twit.'

'We got cut off, didn't we? I was just going to let you know that I can catch a train for Wimford in half an hour. You needn't bother to send the car for me. I don't want to put you out. I'll get a taxi. I expect that you can lend me the fare——'

'I'll lend you my right foot!' said Harry, fiercely.

'Now there's no need to be like that,' Bunter said, reproachfully. 'There's no need to be stuffy. You ought to have known that I was making a joke about oiks when I was in Mauly's study. I don't mind if that's what you are. Live and let live, that's what I say.'

'Blockhead!'

Billy Bunter yapped on. 'And I don't mind putting up with your uncle and aunt, really I don't. He can't help being boring. It'll be a bit dreary for you until I arrive. I know he puts a damper on things but——'

'What?' gasped Harry.

'A silly old fogey, really. But still, I've put up with him before and I'm ready to do it again. There's no need to worry on that score.'

'What a pity you aren't here,' said Harry.

'Oh!' Bunter sounded pleased. He had missed the note of

menace in Harry's voice. 'Do you really, old chap?'

'Then I'd have the pleasure of kicking you all the way home again.'

'But – but――'

'Ring off, you fat freak! I don't want to hear another squeak from you. It'll be bad enough having to listen to your bleat all through next term without having to put up with it in the holidays.'

'Tee, hee, hee!' chuckled the Owl.

'What are you tee-heeing for, you bloated balloon?' demanded Harry.

'Just laughing at your little joke, old man. There's nothing like a sense of humour. But still, I can't stand around chatting. I'll have to get my skates on, or I shall miss that train. I don't want to disappoint you. A promise is a promise.'

'That's right,' Harry agreed. 'A promise is a promise, and I promise that I'll keep a sharp eye open for you.'

'Good.'

'And as soon as we spot you, we'll boot you all the way back to Wimford station, and then we'll boot you into the train just to make sure that you don't miss it.'

'Beast!' shouted Bunter, as Harry banged down the receiver.

Bob came into the hall. 'Come on, Harry,' he said, impatiently. 'We're ready. Have you got your skates?'

'I won't be a moment.' Harry stood by the telephone for another couple of minutes just in case Bunter rang back again, but it remained silent. He sighed with relief. It seemed that this time the fat Owl really had got the message.

CHAPTER 11
Home for the Hols

'Beast!'

Billy Bunter stood by the telephone, a disgruntled expression on his face. He'd made a special effort to ring Wharton that morning, and Wharton hadn't appreciated it. He'd rolled out of bed and had staggered downstairs at an early hour just to have a friendly chinwag, and his friendship had been rejected.

It seemed that it was Bunter Villa for Christmas after all, and that was a depressing thought. The truth was, his family home wasn't quite the grand establishment that he boasted about.

Bunter Villa existed. Bunter Court did not. It was true that they had a cleaner, and a part-time gardener, but they hardly constituted the hordes of well-trained servants he had so often described, and the family car was a humble saloon and not a glittering Rolls. No, he wasn't going to have the luxurious Christmas that he yearned for.

Billy Bunter was equally depressed by the thought of having to put up with his brother and sister. Sammy, for example, had the most irritating habit of snatching the best titbits before he could get his paws on them himself, and Bessie maddened him by harking on and on about some cash he'd borrowed from her some time ago.

There was something else, and the thought of it made the Owl shudder. His father actually expected him to lend a hand about the house. He groaned as he made his way into the living room. It was a grim prospect.

He settled down in a deep armchair by the fire, and put his feet up on the fender, hoping that no one would want him. It was not even eleven o'clock yet – far too early to do anything but rest. However, he wasn't allowed to take it easy for long.

'William!' His father opened the door of the living room.

Billy Bunter huddled up, trying not to breathe too hard, hoping that his father wouldn't know he was there. Perhaps the high back of the armchair, would hide him.

'William!' His father sounded annoyed.

William George remained silent. He was fairly sure that whatever his father wanted him for, it would mean leaving that blazing fire, and undertaking some beastly task.

'William!' His father strode across the room, and glared down.

'Oh – oh!' Billy Bunter looked up. 'Did you want me, father?'

'You know perfectly well that I did. Why didn't you answer?'

'But – but I – I wasn't sure that I heard properly. Anyway, I was just going to get up, and then——'

Mr Bunter looked at him sternly. 'I have just had a word with cook. She says that a cake has disappeared from her kitchen. Do you know anything about it?'

'Me? Of course, not, father. I didn't go anywhere near the kitchen. Wouldn't. If she says she saw me, she's wrong, because she wasn't even there. It wasn't much of a cake anyway. She's always stingy with fruit——'

Mr Bunter went almost purple with fury. 'I've got a good mind to box your ears!'

The Owl blinked up apprehensively, and sank a little lower into the chair. 'Oh, crikey! I – I——'

'I've never met such a greedy boy in my life! Greedy and lazy! What do you think you're doing here? I told you at breakfast to sweep the snow from the garden path.'

'Oh, lor'!'

His father loomed over him, and shook an angry finger. 'Had you forgotten what I said?'

'Oh! Well, yes – that is, no. Well, maybe –' Bunter hadn't forgotten, but he wasn't sure which was the better answer.

'Then get up and do it!' snapped his father. 'I want to be able to see every square inch of the path. Start at the front door, and then work your way down to the front gate.'

'But——'

'And then you can clear the drive up to the garage. I want it completed by lunch time.'

The Owl was appalled at the magnitude of the task. 'What – what about the gardener? Why can't he do it?'

His father gave an exasperated snort. 'For the simple reason that he comes only twice a week, and he doesn't happen to be here today. What is more, I've no intention of paying a man to do something which you are perfectly capable of doing. You could do with a bit of exercise instead of slouching over the fire.'

'But – but it's jolly cold out there, and the sky's got awfully grey. It looks as if it's going to snow again any moment now.

What's the point of sweeping up the beastly stuff if the paths are going to get plastered with it again? Don't make sense.'

'Don't you tell me what makes sense and what doesn't! I want to see you hard at work within five minutes. And I'll tell you something, William. Unless you complete the job, there'll be no lunch for you.'

Bunter's jaw dropped. 'Nun – nunno——'

'No lunch!' repeated his father. Now go and get the broom from the garden shed. Hurry up!'

'Oh!' Bunter almost bounded from the armchair. Anything was better than going without his grub. 'All right, father. Straight away, father.'

He went into the hall, grabbed a pair of gloves, wound a scarf round his neck, and trudged out into the cold. His father had been right about one thing. Exercise was what he needed, but it wasn't what he wanted.

Although it was freezing outside, it wasn't long before there were beads of perspiration on his fat brow. Every now and again, he stopped, leaning on the broom handle and panting loudly, and then, sighing again, he went back to his task.

It took him quite a long time to finish it. Several times he thought that he had come to the end, but each time his father appeared and pointed to the small mounds of snow that he had ignored.

At last it was done, but it gave him no feeling of satisfaction. The sky was heavy with low, grey clouds. The snow would be falling again before very long, and that would mean that he would have to do the same beastly job all over again.

At lunch time, he munched away, his face gloomy. Life in Bunter Villa looked like being even worse than he had anticipated. His mind flashed to thoughts of Wharton Lodge. It would be different there. He wondered what the prospects of a warm welcome would be if he just turned up. Not too good, he suspected, judging by that phone call. But still, there was always a faint hope that things might have changed by the time he got there. He looked at his father, and knew that there was no hope at all of things changing in Bunter Villa. No, Wharton Lodge seemed the better bet.

After lunch when the house was quiet, the Owl sneaked out and made his way to the station. The sky was a dull grey, and it felt very cold indeed. By the time the train reached Wimford, it had started to snow. The flakes were still light and feathery, but he felt it would be coming down heavily before long. Sighing to himself, the Owl trudged off down the road to Wharton Lodge.

Meanwhile the Famous Five had been having a marvellous time. They spent the whole morning skating and had come in to a magnificent lunch. Now they were gathered in Harry's comfortable sitting room. A log fire was crackling in the grate, and the firelight was reflected in the frosty windows.

Bob was standing at the french windows which led on to a small balcony. 'Isn't it smashing!' he exclaimed.

'Indeed it is,' said Hurree Singh, joining him, 'but it looks very cold.'

'Oh, rot!' said Bob. 'Let's go out.'

Hurree shuddered. 'Must we?' he murmured.

'Of course we must,' said Johnny. 'We can't waste all that snow.'

'I can think of a way of using it,' said Frank.

'That's that, Hurree. It's four to one. You're out-voted,' said Harry.

Hurree made a face. 'There are disadvantages in living in a democracy,' he said.

'Let's get our anoraks.' Bob turned to Hurree. 'You can always wrap yourself in a couple of blankets.'

'My dear Bob, you have forgotten. I am Indian, not a Red Indian.'

'Let's get our coats.'

They hurried to their rooms and soon returned. 'Where's Harry?' asked Bob, as he shoved a woolly hat on to his head.

'Here.' Harry came out of the communicating door to his bedroom. As he opened the french windows on to the balcony, a small cloud of snowflakes gusted in.

'It's great!' said Bob, going out. 'Race you to the oak tree!' he yelled.

'Watch it!' said Harry, as Bob made for the flight of steps

59

that led to the garden. 'It's icy!'

He was too late. As Bob raced down, his feet slithered, and he tumbled to the bottom of the steps, a look of utter surprise on his face. 'Crumpets! That hurt!'

'Ha, ha, ha!' roared his friends.

Johnny made his way down, and stretched out a friendly hand.

'Ugh!' spluttered Bob, as that friendly hand pushed his head into a pile of snow. 'Idiot!'

'Follow my leader, is it?' asked Frank, and he followed Johnny's example.

'Wah!' Bob lifted his head from the little drift and wiped some of the snow away. 'Fathead!'

'My turn!' Hurree Singh approached his victim, but he grabbed a handful of snow and sprinkled it over Bob.

'You've got it wrong!' Harry Wharton showed him what to do.

'Clots!' Bob struggled to his feet, looking a bit like a snowman. 'Which of you clowns has got my hat?'

Hurree pointed a finger at him. 'There's the clown.'

'Oh!' As Bob took his great foot off the hat, and bent down to pick it up, Johnny fired a salvo of snowballs at him. He rushed away, turned and fired another which caught Frank Nugent on the ear.

'Twit!' shouted Frank, packing a fistful of snow into a ball.

Before long the air was full of exploding snowballs, and the battle raged. Soon they were all caked in snow. Eventually Frank stopped and leaned against a tree. 'Can't go on,' he gasped. 'Must have a breather,' and the rest of the Famous Five wandered across, and joined him.

Hurree Singh brushed some snow from his black hair, and as he straightened up, he gave a gasp. 'I can hardly believe it!' he exclaimed.

'Believe what?' asked Johnny.

'Look!' Hurree pointed towards the drive.

They all swung round. There, rolling through the gates, was a rotund figure, whose fat little legs clad in tight checked trousers were propelling him towards the Famous Five.

CHAPTER 12
Any Port in a Storm!

'It's Bunter!'
  'He's got a cheek!'
  'What a nerve!'
  'He's got a hide like a rhinoceros!' declared Harry.
  'I say, you fellows!'
  'You've come just at the right moment, fat man!' roared Johnny Bull.
  'Really?' The Owl sounded delighted.
  'Yes. I couldn't think what to do with this.' Johnny picked up a snowball from the pile of ammunition at his feet, and fired it at Billy Bunter.
  'I've got a present too!' Bob Cherry hurled his missile so accurately that it exploded on Bunter's chin.
  Within seconds a hail of smashing, crashing snowballs burst around Bunter who slithered and slipped in the snow.
  'Ooogh! I say – grrruph! I just looked in on the off – agh! Beasts! Wanted to see how – oh, doughnuts! Wug! Wah! Woogh!' The doubts he had had about his reception at Wharton Lodge were dispelled. The storm of snowballs made it quite clear that he wasn't the welcome figure he had hoped to be. Groaning and moaning, he made his way towards the gates.
  'Cheerio!' shouted Bob.
  'Don't go!' bawled Johnny. 'I've only just got my eye in.'
  Billy Bunter turned round. 'Beasts!' he yelled, and then he fled along the Wimford road as fast as his fat, little legs could carry him, and he kept on running until he was out of breath.
  Panting loudly, he leaned against a snow-laden tree, and groaned. 'Oh, lor'!' he mumbled to himself. 'Oh, lor'!' Actually, he hadn't run very far. His plump legs were unused to exercise, and although they had carried him from the

station to the house, they weren't ready to carry him back again yet.

Now he'd been landed with another problem. He had used all the cash he possessed to buy a single ticket to Wimford. How on earth could he get back to Bunter Villa without any money? Not that he was keen to return. He'd left his father a note to say that he'd accepted a pressing invitation from Wharton, and it would be difficult to explain what had happened.

So there he stood, beneath a tree, trying to decide what to do. 'Beasts!' he mumbled. 'Beasts!'

He knew what he wanted, but he didn't know how to do it. What he wanted was to stay at Wharton Lodge, but he had a shrewd idea of what would happen if he marched up the drive to the front door and rang the bell.

He leaned against a wall, and looked up at it. It was part of the stone wall that surrounded the grounds of the house. As he stared at it, a brilliant idea came into his head. Why bother with the front door? There were those stone steps that led into Harry's quarters. He could get in that way. It ought to be safe enough. Those beasts would stay outside until it got dark. All he had to do was to find somewhere to hide.

Still he hesitated. If he was found, he wasn't likely to be welcomed as a guest. They'd boot him back to Wimford station as they'd threatened. On the other hand, provided he managed to keep out of sight for a bit, they might have a change of heart, especially with Christmas Day looming up. It was hard to picture the Famous Five beaming with delight when he revealed himself, but it was better than picturing his father's face if he returned home. Anyway, he hadn't much choice. He couldn't get back without the train fare.

Billy Bunter turned round and stared doubtfully at the wall. It seemed very high to him. He wandered alongside it until he found a section that appeared to be a little lower, and decided he might manage to scramble over it. He stepped back into the road, trotted forward, gave a pathetic little jump in the air, and fell back into the snow. 'Oh, crikey!' he cried.

He made another attempt. This time he managed to grip the top of the wall, and clawed his way up. Once there, he wobbled precariously backwards and forwards. 'Crumbs!' he wailed, and then, with a despairing cry, he fell down into the snow.

'Ugh!' he mumbled. 'Ouch!' He was cold and he was wet, but at least he had landed on the right side of the wall. He could hear faint cries and bursts of laugher coming from some distance away. 'Good!' he said. Those beasts were still outside the house.

He brushed aside snow-covered leaves, and peered through the shrubbery. There seemed to be no one in sight, and so he made his way cautiously from one clump of bushes to another, working his way around the house until he was opposite the steps that led to Harry's rooms. He parted some branches, poked his fat head between them, and looked around again.

There was still no one to be seen. He noticed the smooth layer of snow on the lawn. He would have to cross it, but his footsteps wouldn't be visible for long. The falling snow would obliterate them.

He wriggled his way out of the shrubbery, stole stealthily across the grass, slipped up to the balcony, and tiptoed into Harry's den. As he opened the door, a wild flurry of snow was blown in with him, and chunks fell from his body, dropping soggily on to the floor.

Bunter clapped his hands to his mouth. His trial outside would soon be hidden by the fast-falling flakes, but it was different here. It would give the game away. Then inspiration struck. He threw the french windows wide open, sniggering to himself as gusts of wind blew in yet more snow. The Famous Five would simply think that they hadn't closed the door properly.

He stared round the room. As usual, it was warm and comfortable, and he was tempted to settle down by the crackling fire, but he knew that it would be fatal. Once down, it would be difficult to get up, and it was essential to find a hiding place as soon as possible.

He made his way towards the door that led to the corridor, but then, out of the corner of his eye, he caught sight of a large bowl of fruit on the table. He rubbed his hands together at the sight of all those oranges, apples, tangerines and bananas.

'What a bit of luck!' he breathed. His eager paws shot out, and within seconds, the dish was empty and his pockets were full. His eyes gleamed with satisfaction. Yet another problem had been solved. At least he wasn't going to starve.

Quietly, he turned the door handle, and poked his head round the corner of the door, looking first one way and then the other. Since there wasn't anyone in sight and not a sound to be heard, he slipped out, and then stood quite still.

To his left, the corridor ended in a gallery which overlooked the hall. To the right, it led away past the bedrooms. At the far end, he now recalled, there was a narrow, winding staircase that led up to a disused attic. That, he realized, was his best bet. An attic was hardly his idea of a comfortable hideout, but it was the best that he could hope for.

As silently as possible, he made his way along the broad corridor, hurried up the dark, twisting stairs, pushed open the door, and stared in at his new home. 'Oh, crikey!' he squeaked, in dismay.

It had a small, dusty window which let in just enough light for him to see what the room was like. Judging by the dust and the musty smell, it hadn't been used for years. There was a large old fireplace, and in the alcove on one side was a cracked, yellow sink with an ancient cold water tap. On the other side was a sagging iron bedstead with an old mattress. A dusty square of carpet covered most of the floor, and there were a few old boxes, a worm-eaten wash-stand, and a few other bits of rubbish abandond there.

'Oh, crikey!' he repeated. The attic was a refuge, all right, but not a very inviting one. However, it would have to do. At least it would be safe. He couldn't believe that anyone would go all the way up those stairs just to look at it, and so he bowled in, and shut the door.

Although his future was far from certain, Billy Bunter was not displeased with himself. He plonked himself on the edge of the rickety bed, and began to sort out the fruit. He was perfectly contented. After all, he'd got food and shelter. What more could anyone want?

CHAPTER 13
Strange Intruder

'I'm flaked!' announced Frank Nugent.

Bob gave him a broad grin. 'You look it,' he said. 'You're covered in snow.'

'We're all covered in it,' said Harry. 'Let's pack it in.'

As they made their way back to the house, it was already beginning to get dark, and it was snowing so heavily that the imprints made by their feet as they trotted across the lawn were soon filled in.

Bob Cherry reached the steps ahead of the others, and trampled up to the balcony. 'Hallo!' he said, surprised at seeing the french windows open. 'We couldn't have fastened the door properly –' He broke off, a look of astonishment on his face. Just inside the room and standing with his back to the door was a slight figure wearing a thick overcoat with a peaked black cap pulled low over his head. 'What the thump——?'

At the sound of Bob's voice, the figure swung round. A man stared at him for just a second, his narrow, dark eyes glittering, and then, without a moment's hesitation, he lowered his head and launched himself at Bob.

'Ouch!' cried Bob, as a hard head knocked all the breath from his body, and he stumbled back on to the balcony, slithered, and then slipped.

The intruder staggered under the impact, but he steadied himself and gripped the edge of the balcony, glaring furiously at the sight of three more boys coming up the steps.

Bob made a feeble effort to grasp the man's leg, but his hand was knocked aside, and the intruder hurtled recklessly down the steps, pushing with rough hands at Hurree so that he slipped backwards on to Johnny, who then crashed into Frank, so that all three landed in a tangled heap in the snow.

The man neatly sprang over them, and then sped off into the gathering gloom.

Harry, who had lingered behind to look for a glove, came across the lawn. 'Haven't you had enough?' he asked in an amused tone, seeing Hurree, Frank and Johnny rolling around.

Johnny wriggled out from underneath Hurree and Frank. 'What was all that about?'

Bob Cherry, now on his feet, leaned over the balcony. 'Did you get a look at him? He winded me.'

'And Johnny winded me,' said Frank, struggling up.

Harry looked puzzled. 'What's been going on?'

Bob clattered down. 'There was some bloke in your room. As soon as he saw me, he shot off——'

'Went down the steps like greased lightning,' added Johnny. 'We went down like ninepins——'

'He leaped over us, and whizzed off,' said Frank.

Harry stared around. 'Well, he's got away. There's no point in going after him now.'

'But who do you think it was?' asked Frank.

Harry shrugged. 'Search me.'

'It must have been a tramp,' growled Johnny.

'Or another burglar?' suggested Hurree.

'Not very lightly,' said Harry. 'Lightning doesn't strike twice,' but he looked worried. 'It was much more likely to have been a tramp as Johnny said.'

'I doubt it,' said Hurree, thoughtfully. 'Surely a tramp would be tucked up in some nice warm barn by now.'

'It's no good standing around here in the cold,' said Harry. 'Let's have a look inside.' He stepped into the room and switched on the light. 'Cripes!' he said. 'Look at that!' There was snow everywhere.

Bob strode in. 'I don't think he'd been here more than a minute or two. He wasn't doing anything. He was standing with his back to the balcony, looking at the door to the corridor.'

'He must have been here for some time,' argued Frank, 'or else there wouldn't be so much snow in the room.'

'But if we'd left it open when we went out, there would have

66

The man sprang neatly over them.

been plenty of time for it to pile up.'

Frank turned to Harry, who was prowling round the room. 'Is anything missing?' he asked.

Harry shook his head. 'I don't think so, but you'd better go and look in your own rooms. If he was a tramp, I guess he'd have been after cash rather than anything else.'

'I say, Harry!' exclaimed Bob. 'Something is missing.'

'Oh?' Harry turned to him.

Bob pointed towards the table. 'He must have been starving.'

'Oh! The fruit! It's gone!'

'Now that really is quite extraordinary,' said Hurree. 'There's nothing left, and yet there isn't an apple core or a banana skin in sight.'

'He must have shoved it into his pockets,' Frank said.

'Why do that when you can stuff them with cash and bits of silver?' asked Bob.

'It was a tramp,' said Johnny, obstinately.

'Let's go and look in our rooms like Harry said,' suggested Bob. 'Then we'll give you a hand to clear up.'

'Thanks,' said Harry, gratefully. 'Aunt Amy's a bit short-handed at the moment. It won't be so bad tomorrow. John, the gardener's boy, is going to lend a hand since there isn't much he can do outside.'

They all shot into their rooms, and were back within minutes. 'All correct,' announced Bob. 'Everything's ship-shape.'

There was a murmur of agreement, and Harry's face cleared. 'Good,' he said. 'I'll just nip downstairs and tell my uncle about it, but I think we'll have to lock that door from now on. It's an open invitation to anyone who's prowling about.'

'It really is curious,' said Hurree. 'Fancy going to all that trouble to break in, and to take nothing but fruit.'

'Oh, well,' said Frank, 'I only hope he enjoys it.'

He did. Up in the attic Billy Bunter enjoyed every mouthful of apple, every bite of banana, and every slice of tangerine, but once they were gone he realized that he wasn't enjoying

68

anything else very much. He was uncomfortable, and he was also very cold.

He sat on the edge of the bed, hugging his coat tightly round himself, and shivered, feeling quite, quite miserable. It was now very dark, and there was nothing but the glimmer of snow outside, and the faint gleam of wintry starlight.

He began to think he would freeze to death. Something had to be done, but what? There were plenty of blankets in Wharton Lodge, but how was he to lay his hands on them? He had got away with the disappearance of the fruit – after all, anyone might have helped himself to that, but the disappearance of blankets would be another kettle of fish.

The Owl thought it over, and after a time, he began to chuckle. Suppose Wharton walked into his bedroom and found it shipped – what would he think? He'd think one of his friends had done it for a lark. He'd probably blame Cherry, but he wouldn't tell the Colonel about it. Bunter chuckled again so that the bed began to creak. Yes, that was the answer. He'd wreck Wharton's bed.

He got up, and the bedsprings groaned in relief. Guessing that everyone would be downstairs, he opened the attic door, and listened intently. There was only silence.

Cautiously, he crept down the narrow stairs to the last bend of the staircase, and poked his head round the corner. He took two more steps, and peeped into the corridor.

The bedroom doors were closed, but he thought he heard faint sounds coming from one of them, and he retreated again. There was the click of a door, and the rapid clattering of heels along the corridor and down the main staircase.

Billy Bunter waited for another couple of minutes, and then ventured down, glinting first one way and then the other. He tiptoed towards the gallery that overlooked the hall, and listened. There was a tinkling of a piano.

'Come on, Frank! Let's have it again!' Bob Cherry said.

'That's right, m'boys. Make it a really rousing chorus this time.' Bunter knew that gruff voice. It was Colonel Wharton speaking.

Five voices roared out a favourite Christmas carol. 'Good King Wenceslas looked out,' they sang.

Billy Bunter didn't think that he'd bother to hear any more. He wasn't interested in that good old man or anyone else, come to that. Neither was he interested in the page and his cold feet. He only knew that he was going to make sure that he didn't get into the same state.

He risked a glance into the hall below. The oak panelling was decorated with holly and mistletoe. There was a log fire blazing away, and the Colonel was standing with his back to it, his ruddy face beaming with pleasure. His wife was sitting in a comfortable armchair on one side of the fire, her foot beating time to the music, while Frank was at the piano with the others gathered around him.

Bunter felt reassured at the scene. They looked as if they were in for a good long session, and no doubt there would still be supper to come. There should be plenty of time for him to carry out his little plan.

He padded back along the corridor, and slipped into Harry's room. His little eyes glittered as he spotted the fruit dish. The last time he had seen it, it had been empty. Now someone had thoughtfully filled it up again. Once more he shovelled its contents into his pockets, and then he went into Harry's bedroom.

He looked around, and quickly ripped the quilt and the blankets from the bed and put them in a pile by the door. Next he pulled the sheets from the bed, rolled them into a ball, and hurled then across the room.

Chuckling away, he grabbed the mattress, and flung it over the end of the bed, putting a couple of chairs in its place. Then he flung open the wardrobe, snatched some of Harry's clothes from their hangers, and tossed them around the room. Finally, he put Harry's brush and comb in his shoes.

He blinked around the room, wondering if there was anything else that he could do. A brilliant idea came into his head, and he clambered on to the bed, half opened the door, and balanced a pillow on top of it. When Harry opened the door, it would come crashing down on his head.

Billy Bunter tittered to himself as he took the other pillow for his own use. He bent down, picked up the rest of his bedding, and pushed open the door.

70

There was a thud. 'Ug! Wug! Crikey!' The Owl had been caught in his own trap. Crossly, he picked up the pillow that had thumped him, hurled it on top of the wardrobe, and crept off to his refuge once again.

CHAPTER 14

A Mystery

'Goodnight, Mrs Wharton. Goodnight, Colonel Wharton!' Supper was over, and the Famous Five were on their way to bed.

'Sleep well,' said Aunt Amy.

'It was a smashing evening,' said Bob, and the others murmured in agreement.

Harry lingered for a few moments after the others had left. 'It's good to be home,' he said, and the Colonel's face beamed with pleasure.

'Glad of that, m'boy,' he said, as Harry left the room.

Harry ran up the stairs, wandered into his sitting room, and stood by glowing embers of the fire, thinking of his uncle and aunt's kindness, and of the welcome they had given his friends. 'Ah, well,' he said to himself, 'I guess I'd better go to bed too.'

He pushed the door of his room wide open and stood in the doorway, rooted to the spot. 'Oh, jeepers!' he exclaimed. He could hardly believe his eyes. His room was a total wreck. He didn't mind practical jokes, but this just wasn't funny. Someone had gone too far.

Harry Wharton bit his lip, and frowned. He could guess who that someone was. Bob Cherry was known for his high spirits, but occasionally those high spirits got out of hand.

It couldn't be any of the others. Frank Nugent was too thoughtful, Johnny Bull had too much common sense, and Hurree Jamset Ram Singh would consider it bad taste. No, he decided, it was Bob Cherry all right.

'Fool!' he said, as he began to straighten up his room.

Although he was annoyed, he decided not to kick up a fuss about it. After all, Christmas was Christmas.

He wandered slowly round the room, picked up his clothes and hung them up again, removed the chairs from the bed, and rolled back the mattress. It was only then that he realized that the bedding had gone. 'Stupid clot!' he said crossly, and began to search for it.

Ten minutes later, he stood in the middle of the bedroom, his hands on his hips, and a look of exasperation on his face. He'd looked everywhere – in the wardrobe, in drawers, under the bed, and in his den, and all he'd found was a solitary pillow. Now what was he going to do? It was a cold night, and he wanted those blankets and that quilt. Well, there was nothing for it but to go and see Bob.

He stomped along the corridor, and tapped on Bob's door. 'Are you in bed yet?'

'No. Come in, Harry.' Bob was standing by his dressing table, his sweater in his hands. 'Is anything wrong?' he asked, noticing Harry's eyes flickering around the room.

'I wouldn't actually say that there's anything wrong,' said Harry, trying to sound casual. 'It's just that something's not quite right.'

'Oh?'

Harry changed the subject. 'It's a bit nippy tonight, isn't it?'

'Nippy? That's putting it mildly. It's positively perishing.'

'That's why I want my blankets.'

Bob looked puzzled. 'Your what?'

'My blankets,' repeated Harry, patiently. 'I've got a feeling that I'm going to need them – and my quilt.'

Bob ran his hands through his hair. 'What are you on about, Harry?' he asked.

'Don't you know?'

'I haven't a clue. What are you getting at?'

'I've told you. I want my blankets back.'

'Why come here?'

'Because they're not on my bed. Where are they?'

'How the dickens should I know?' demanded Bob. 'I haven't got a crystal ball. It's nothing to do with me.'

'Isn't it?' said Harry drily. 'Listen, Bob. A joke's a joke, and

72

you've had a laugh, but I reckon it's over now. So can I have them back, please?'

Bob looked astonished. 'Somebody's snitched them, is that what you're saying?'

'That's right. My room's been shipped – no, it's worse than that. It's been wrecked, and practically all of the bedclothes have vanished.'

Bob's face went red. 'And you thought it was me? I know that I go in for practical jokes now and again, Harry, but I know where to draw the line. I'm a guest here. I wouldn't dream of doing anything like that.'

'No?'

'No!' Bob began to sound angry. 'I can't think why you asked me here if you thought I wouldn't know how to behave.'

Harry's conviction that it was Bob who'd wrecked his room began to ebb. 'I'm – I'm sorry, Bob. It was just that I remembered the time you shipped Loder's bed, and you made a thorough job of that.'

'And that made you think that I'd do the same to you?'

'Well——'

'You haven't got much of an opinion of me, have you?'

'I realized it would only be a joke,' said Harry awkwardly.

'It doesn't sound much like a joke.'

'I know, but someone has——'

Bob interrupted him. 'It wasn't me,' he said, flatly.

'If you say it wasn't you, then it wasn't you. I'm sorry, Bob, but I simply thought that maybe——'

'Then you thought wrong. You can search the room if you like.'

'Don't be an ass, Bob. I wouldn't do that.'

'You'll have to look elsewhere then. You don't suppose that Tom Wells has gone off his head and whipped them, do you?'

'Of course he hasn't.'

'Somebody else on the staff?'

'No,' said Harry.

Bob sat on his bed, and took off his shoes. 'Sorry, but I can't help.'

'Okay. Goodnight, Bob.'

73

'Goodnight,' said Bob, hardly bothering to look at him.

Harry left the room and shut the door, and stood in the corridor thinking for a minute or two. No one who worked in the house would do it. It was much more likely to be one of his friends, but which one? Bob was certainly the most likely candidate but if he had been guilty, he'd have said so.

Harry heaved a sigh, and tapped at the next door. As Frank, already wearing pyjamas, opened the door, he said, 'Sorry to bother you, Frank, but – well, I just wondered——'

Frank took one look at Harry's face. 'What's up?' he said, quickly.

Harry managed a faint smile. 'Some twit has pinched the blankets from my bed. I take it you're not the twit, Frank?'

'No. Not guilty.'

'I didn't think you would be.'

'Why not ask Bob?'

'I have. He says he doesn't know anything about it.'

'If he says he hasn't, then he hasn't.'

'I know. Well, I'll have to ask Johnny and Hurree, but it doesn't sound like them, does it?'

Frank shook his head. 'No.'

'But still, I'll have to ask. I want those blankets. I need them. I can't bother my aunt at this time of night, and anyway, I don't really want her to know about it. Oh, well, I guess I'll find them. Goodnight, Frank.'

'Goodnight. Good hunting.'

As Frank shut his door, Johnny came out of the bathroom. 'What's wrong with you?' he asked, looking at Harry's face.

'Somebody's turned my room upside down and pinched my bedclothes.'

'Asked Bob?'

'Yes, but he said that he didn't do it, and neither did Frank.'

Johnny's face went a dull red. 'You don't think it was me, do you?' he said, grimly.

'Oh, no. I just thought I'd ask.'

'I wouldn't behave like that in another fellow's house.'

'I know, but——'

'So why are you asking me?' Johnny marched into his

74

room, and banged the door.

'What's going on?' Hurree Singh's dark face appeared round the corner of his door.

'Someone's played an idiotic joke on me. My room's been wrecked, and my bedclothes are missing. Do you know anything about it, Hurree?'

Hurree shook his head. 'I don't go in for wrecking rooms and stealing bedclothes.'

'I know you don't.'

'Have you asked Bob?'

Although he was fed up, Harry couldn't help smiling. Poor old Bob. He seemed to be everyone's prime suspect. 'He said he hadn't anything to do with it. Never mind, Hurree. I'll manage somehow. It'll get sorted out in the morning.'

'Would you like to share my bedclothes?'

'No, it'll be all right.'

'Sure?'

'Sure. Goodnight, Hurree.'

'Goodnight.'

Harry returned to his own room. The whole thing was a mystery. Somebody had done it. The blankets hadn't just walked off on their own, but no one had come clean. Sighing wearily, he pulled his overcoat and raincoat from the wardrobe, picked up a rug, threw them on the bed, and looked doubtfully at it. He wasn't going to have a very comfortable night. He fancied it would be some time before he dropped off to sleep.

Billy Bunter had had no such problem. He was already slumbering in his remote attic, warmly wrapped in Harry's bedclothes.

CHAPTER 15
Narrow Escape

When Billy Bunter woke up the next morning, the first glimmer of a grey, December dawn was showing through the small, dusty attic window. As he sat up and rubbed his eyes, the old iron bedstead creaked under his weight.

He seldom woke as early as this, but his stomach acted as a kind of watchdog, and although he had been soundly asleep, it had sounded the alarm. It was empty, and so he woke up, immediately aware of the aching void. He was ravenous. It was true that he had had the fruit, but that had soon disappeared, and all that was left was a mound of peel, banana skins, and apple cores.

'Oh, crumbs!' he groaned, as he rolled off the bed.

He was an unattractive sight by now. He had slept in his clothes, his hair stuck up in the air, and his face was dirty and sticky, but even if he had known, he wouldn't have cared. There was something much more important than the way he looked, and that was breakfast. Food was essential, washing was not. He had to do something about it, and he had to do it soon.

As silently as possible, he opened the attic door and peered down the dim, shadowy stairs. Although he hadn't the slightest idea of the time, he was fairly certain that it was early. With any luck, no one would be about. He'd be able to forage around and pick up supplies for the day.

He followed his usual routine going down the stairs, and once he saw that the coast was clear, he padded along the shadowy, silent corridor to Harry's sitting room. He directed his gaze towards the table.

'Beasts!' he hissed. The fruit dish was just the way that he had left it – empty.

Crossly, he closed the door again and tiptoed along to the

76

gallery overlooking the hall. He put both hands on the ledge, leaned over, and looked down. It was empty. Taking his courage in both hands, he made his way down the stairs. If anyone came along, he'd have no chance of escape. He'd be caught – caught and returned to Bunter Villa!

His heart was pounding by the time he reached the bottom of the staircase, and it pounded even more as he made his way across to the door that led to the kitchen. By now, in spite of his fear, his eyes were gleaming. Soon his hands would be busy, doing the work they liked best – transferring food from one container into another. He leaned against the kitchen door, his fat ears strained for the slightest sound, and then his face paled. He could hear footsteps on the other side of the door.

He let out a groan, and his stomach rumbled in sympathy. What could he do? The kitchen was barred to him. He blinked around, and then a fat grin spread across his face. The dining room! There always used to be a large box of biscuits kept in the heavy old sideboard. Mrs Wharton probably still kept one there. A couple of pounds of biscuits would be better than nothing.

He slipped across the hall, and softly slid inside the room. It was dark in there, with blinds pulled down over the three tall windows. Leaving the door open so that light from the hall filtered in, he crept swiftly to the sideboard, and looked inside.

A grin spread across his fat face. There, just as he had hoped, was a large box of biscuits. Within seconds, he was munching and crunching, and as he munched and crunched, he crammed handfuls of biscuits into his pockets, dropping some on to the floor in his eagerness to get his fat paws on them. A little later, he dipped into the tin again, and a look of surprise spread across his face. The box was empty.

He was just about to leave the room, when he noticed the biscuits on the floor. As he bent down to pick them up, the dining room door was pushed wide open, and a short, erect figure came in. Bunter goggled. It was Tom Wells.

Had the fat Owl been upright, Tom Wells would have seen him in spite of the dimness, but he was safely concealed by the dining room table.

Wells marched across to the window, fiddled with a blind, and it shot up, so that wintery light streamed in.

'Oh, choc drops!' said Bunter to himself. He wasn't going to be concealed for long.

As Wells moved on to the second window, the Owl crept on his hands and knees towards the door, but he was slow off the mark and he hadn't reached it by the time the second blind swished up.

As Wells made his way to the third blind, Bunter slunk outside, but at the same time there was a sudden swish, and the Owl's heart sank. If Wells came straight out into the hall, he'd be seen. There was nowhere to hide, and he couldn't hope to get up the stairs in time.

There was a grunt from inside the dining room. 'What are all those crumbs doing on the floor?' There was another grunt. 'The box is empty! Cleaned out! It's that John, that's who it is. I'll speak to him. It's not the first time, but it had better be that last. I'll –' There was a clatter as the box was picked up, and the sideboard door was opened. It was now or never. The fat Owl sped across the hall, and shot up the stairs.

'John? Is that you?'

The Owl rushed along the upstairs corridor, hearing the rapid footsteps of Wells crossing the hall towards the stairs. He knew that he couldn't possibly reach his attic in time, and so he darted into Harry's den, hoping that he was not yet awake, and stood by the door, gulping for breath.

'Where are you, John?' Wells had reached the top of the stairs, and was making his way down the corridor.

Bunter blinked around the room, looking for a good hiding place. There was a large, heavy settee in one corner of the room, and Bunter could see that he might be able to squeeze into the space behind it. He hurried across the room, pitched himself over the top, and collapsed breathlessly into the corner.

He was only just in time. The door opened, and although the Owl couldn't see him, he knew that Tom Wells was inspecting the room. There was a snort, and the door was closed again.

He let out a great, fat sigh of relief. Although he'd have to stay where he was for the time being, at least he was safe.

'Tee, hee, hee!' he tittered. 'Fooled him, the silly ass!' The thought that John was being blamed for the disappearance of the biscuits didn't even enter his head, and even if it had, it wouldn't have bothered him. He'd got away. That was the only thing that counted.

He went on tittering as he dipped his hand in his pocket, and brought out some biscuits. He was still in danger, and he should have been worried, but there was comfort in food and so, as he chewed, his cares slipped away.

It was some time later that he pricked up his ears. 'Beast!' he mumbled. Up till then, the silence had been broken only by the sound of chomping, but now he heard a noise coming from Harry's bedroom. Was that beast getting up? He listened, his ears flapping, but there was silence again.

It was time to make his way back to his attic. Putting both hands on the back of the settee, the Owl levered himself up, but he ducked down again as he saw the door handle turning.

Light footsteps crossed the room, and Bunter squinted from beneath the settee and caught a glimpse of a young boy carrying a basket of logs and a bucket. He scraped away at the grate and cleaned it out, crumpled up newspaper, laid wood on top of it, and then he lit the fire. He stood watching it for a minute or two, and then, satisfied that it was properly alight, he piled the rest of the logs in the fireplace, and left the room.

At last the coast was clear. Once more he put his fat paws on the back of the settee, and once more he sank back again. This time it was because there were voices outside.

'What have you been doing, John?' It was a woman speaking.

'Been lighting the fire, Alice.'

'I don't mean that, stupid. I mean what have you been up to? Mr Wells is after your blood.'

'What for? I haven't done anything.'

'Oh, no? What did you do in the dining room?'

'The dining room? What about it? I haven't been anywhere near it.'

'You were last night.'

'I only made the fire up.' John sounded fed up. 'I'm sick of working inside. I wish I could get out into the garden.'

'You ought to be grateful to the Colonel for finding you something to do.'

'That's what everyone keeps saying.' John didn't sound very grateful. 'Anyway, what does Mr Wells think I was doing in the dining room?'

'It's the biscuits. That box in the sideboard is empty.'

'Well, I don't know anything about it,' cried John indignantly. 'He's just picked on me because I did help myself once, but I owned up when I was asked, and promised I wouldn't do it again, and I haven't. Even if I had, I wouldn't be daft enough to scoff the lot, would I?'

Alice's voice was suspicious. 'Well, I don't know about that, John.'

'Well, I do,' said John, and he clattered off down the stairs.

Any faint hope that Bunter might have had that escape was in sight was shattered as Alice entered Harry's den. She had brought the vacuum cleaner, a duster and some polish, and she set about her work. Billy Bunter bit his lip as he heard the sound of furniture being moved. Would she or wouldn't she move the settee? She didn't. It was very heavy, and she had a great deal to get through that morning, and so she simply plumped up the cushions, and left the room.

Billy Bunter breathed again. His fat, round face rose once more above the back of the settee, and then it disappeared from view as he caught the sound of activity coming from the next room. Harry Wharton really was on the move this time. The fat Owl crouched back in his corner. It was a tight fit and he was feeling cramped, but he huddled down again, dismally aware of the fact that he was stuck. Now he would have to wait until the Famous Five went down to breakfast.

There was activity in the corridor. Doors were being opened and shut, and there was a faint murmur of voices. The fat Owl scowled. Why couldn't they be sensible and stay in bed for half the morning as he would have done? He shook his head. He really didn't understand them.

CHAPTER 16
A View from the Corner

'Hallo, hallo, hallo!' exclaimed Bob, as he entered Harry's den.

The communicating door opened. 'Hi, bob,' said Harry. 'Take a pew. I've asked the others to drop in before they go downstairs.'

Bunter gave a long, inward sigh. The others! That could mean that he'd be stuck in the room for ages while they gabbled away. He went cold as they walked across the room towards the settee. There was a creak of the springs as Bob flung himself down on it. The Owl shuddered. Suppose that beast took it into his head to look over the back! He almost groaned aloud at the thought of the booting he'd receive.

'Morning!' said Frank cheerfully, as he came in with Hurree, closely followed by Johnny.

'Sorry to drag you in here before breakfast,' began Harry.

'What did you want to see us for?' asked Frank. 'It wasn't to discuss the weather, was it?'

'No,' said Harry, sounding awkward. 'It wasn't. It – it was about the mess in my bedroom last night.'

Billy Bunter settled down to listen with interest, a fat grin on his face.

'Did you find your bedclothes?' Frank asked.

Harry shook his head. 'No. I looked everywhere last night, and I've had another search this morning. They've gone – vanished. I know that it was only meant as a practical joke, but——'

'Some joke!' grunted Johnny Bull, and he directed a hard stare at Bob. 'I can only think of one person in this house who'd do something as daft as that.'

Bob jumped up, his face flushed. 'So can I!' he shouted. 'I can think of someone who comes from Yorkshire, someone who's a stubborn——'

'Look here, you southern squit——'

'You watch what you're saying, Bull,' said Bob, furiously, 'or I'll show you what a southerner can do to a northern twit!'

'Hold on!' exclaimed Harry. 'We're not going to get anywhere if we spend all day blaming each other. Listen, Johnny. Bob's already told me that he doesn't know anything about it, and as far as I'm concerned, that's that.'

'Then who else could have done it?' Johnny demanded.

'I haven't a clue.'

'It's beyond me,' said Frank. 'After all, if it wasn't one of us, who else could it be.'

Billy Bunter, huddled up in his corner, smirked. He'd really put the cat among the pigeons this time.

'It's beyond me too,' agreed Harry. 'It just has to be someone in the house, but none of the staff would have done it. Anyway, the point is, I don't want my uncle and aunt to know. They'd think——'

'That one of us has got rotten bad manners,' said Frank.

'Exactly.'

'I guess you're right, Harry,' muttered Bob. 'Least said, soonest mended, I suppose.'

'Of course we shan't mention it,' said Hurree, 'but what will Alice think when she makes your bed?'

'Nothing. I've thought it out. I shall tell her we need the bedclothes for a charade or something, and ask her to find me some more. If I tell her that we're putting on a show for my uncle and aunt, and that it's a secret, she won't breathe a word. The other stuff will turn up later on, I suppose, and she can bung it back into the cupboard.' He sighed. 'I don't like lying, but I don't want this to get out.'

'Of course not,' said Hurree.

'I don't want anyone thinking——'

'That it was one of us,' Johnny repeated.

As Bob's flush deepened, Harry said quickly, 'That isn't what I was going to say, Johnny.'

'Perhaps not, but it's what I meant. I suppose it's just possible that there's a practical joker hiding in the house, but it doesn't seem very likely, does it?'

'Not really,' admitted Harry, reluctantly.

'There you are then. If it isn't anyone else, then it has to be one of us,' and he gave Bob Cherry another hard stare.

Bob glared back. 'Okay, Bull. Then it's one of us. Who are you pointing the finger at?'

'Why ask me?' growled Johnny. 'You ought to know.'

Bob strode across to him. 'Are you saying that you don't believe me?'

Johnny folded his arms. 'I know you, Bob Cherry. You're a practical joker, and you're always pulling people's legs. You might just be having us on.'

'You stupid clot!' yelled Bob, shaking his fist at Johnny. 'I'm not pulling anyone's leg over this, but if you keep on like this, I'll – I'll – I'll pull your hooter!'

'Just you try!'

Frank got between them. 'Take it easy,' he said. 'Since we know it wasn't one of us——'

'But Johnny said——'

'Use your loaf, Cherry!' grunted Johnny. 'It's got to be someone, hasn't it? Who's the most likely candidate? Who's the practical joker in this crowd? Who——?'

'I'll punch your stupid head in!' shouted Bob.

'A fat lot of good that would do. Why don't you come clean? If you've hidden the blankets, why not come out into the open and say so?'

As Bob launched himself at Johnny, Harry caught his arm. 'Pack that in, Bob. It won't do any good.'

Bob breathed hard. 'All right, Harry. I'm sorry. I'd forgotten where I was. Mind you, if we were back in Greyfriars, I'd give him a hammering. But I want to get something clear. I don't care what he thinks, but I do care about you. If you suspect me, out with it. I'll pack my bags and——'

'You're just being a stupid clot!' said Harry. 'I've already told you that I believe you. So does Johnny,' and he turned and stared at Johnny, daring him to say anything else. As he remained silent, Harry went on, 'It's a mystery, and that's all there is to it. Let's forget it.'

'I couldn't agree more.' Frank got to his feet. 'Let's have a run before breakfast. I reckon we all need some fresh air.'

'Right. That's settled then.' Harry unlocked the door to the balcony, led them out, and then relocked it.

As soon as he heard that welcome sound, Billy Bunter eased himself from his cramped position, and chuckled aloud. 'Tee, hee, hee!'

He was delighted with the way that things had gone. No one had guessed that it was he who had whipped the blankets. He rubbed his fat hands together, a broad grin on his face. The Bunter horizon seemed much brighter. He still hadn't the slightest idea of how and when to reveal himself, but he was convinced that when he did, it would all be all right.

All he had to do was to reach his attic in safety. He could hear Alice still at work in the bedrooms, but at last he heard her going downstairs. He waited for another couple of minutes, massaging his fat, little legs, and then he clambered over the back of the settee. He reached the door just as the handle began to turn.

CHAPTER 17

Mystery of a Cake

The fat Owl shook. There was no time to reach his hiding place – there wasn't even time to think. Instinctively, he backed behind the door, barely repressing an indignant squeak as it bumped against the tip of his fat nose.

Quick, light footsteps crossed the room. Something was placed on the table, the footsteps returned, the door was closed, and whoever it was went away down the corridor.

'Oh!' squeaked Bunter. It had been another narrow escape. He wiped his hand across his brow leaving yet another smudge on his grimy face. He crept out, and blinked towards the table. 'Oh!' He gave a fat smile.

He could hardly believe his luck. There was a large cake standing on a plate. He still had a few biscuits in his pocket, but what were biscuits compared to this magnificent offering? There it stood, dark brown and covered in nuts and cherries, and smelling absolutely delicious. Harry's Aunt Amy understood boys. She knew that they had hearty appetites, and so she had sent it upstairs for elevenses later on, and that, Bunter decided, was what it would be used for – his very own elevenses.

Eyes gleaming, he rolled across to the table. He and the cake would vanish together, and if it was missed, well that would be another little mystery for the Famous Five to puzzle over.

He grabbed the cake, tucked it under his arm, padded across to the door once more, and listened carefully. There wasn't a sound. Cautiously, he opened the door a crack, and peered out.

There was the familiar voice of Tom Wells. 'John!'

'Yes, Mr Wells.' John sounded as if he was on his way downstairs.

'Have you put that cake in the sitting room yet?'

'Yes, just a second ago.'

'Good.'

'Nosey parker!' hissed Bunter. Why couldn't they get on with their work and stop prowling all over the house? His heart sank as he realized that Tom Wells was coming along the corridor. Billy Bunter didn't know what Wells wanted, but he wasn't going to wait and find out. He shot into Harry's bedroom and closed the door, listening anxiously. A few seconds later, Tom Wells walked into the den.

'Huh!'

'Oh, crikey!' thought Bunter. He could guess what Tom Wells was grunting for. He'd come to make sure that John had put the cake on the table, and he'd found out that it was missing.

The fat Owl bent down and peeped through the keyhole. Wells, his hands on his hips, was standing by the table. It was clear that he was very angry. He'd already suspected the boy of taking the biscuits, and now there wasn't a sign of the cake.

'Young blighter!' rumbled Wells. 'Well, he's had it this time. He's gone too far. He's been helping himself again.

He grabbed the cake . . .

Well, now he'll have to pay for it. It'll be the sack for him. We'll see what the Colonel has to say about it. He won't stand for pilfering.' Still rumbling, he stalked out of the room.

'Bubble and squeak!' Billy Bunter was dismayed. He had no scruples about helping himself to other people's grub. Cakes, trifles, fruit, chocolates, meringues, and even dolly mixture were all grist to the Bunter mill, so to speak, but now he felt a twinge of conscience. Cake or no cake, he just couldn't let John be fired.

He held it out at arm's length, and looked lovingly at it. It was a perfect cake, the best cake he had seen in a long, long while, and he could hardly bring himself to part with it. Sadly, he gave it one last glance, opened the door and slipped silently into the living room, and replaced it on the plate. It was just about the most heroic thing that he had ever done in his life.

He backed into the bedroom, his eyes still fixed on it as if to carry its picture in his mind for ever, and then he quietly closed the door. He remained listening, one fat ear pressed to the keyhole, awaiting the return of Wells. He hadn't very long to wait. There were voices in the corridor.

'This is a nasty business. Are you sure it isn't there?' asked Colonel Wharton.

'Certain,' said Tom Wells.

'But I left it there, Colonel Wharton. Honest I did.' Although John's voice was indignant, he sounded as if he was fairly close to tears.

'Then you have nothing to worry about, my boy,' said the Colonel. 'If you put it on the table, then it will still be there.'

Billy Bunter put his eye to the keyhole. The Colonel strode into the room while John hovered in the doorway. There was an exclamation from Colonel Wharton. 'Good gad! You said it wasn't here, Tom!'

'That's right.' Tom stepped into the room, gasped, and came to a halt, a look of utter surprise on his face. 'But – but –' His eyes were bulging as he pointed wordlessly at the cake.

'It's the same one, isn't it?' asked the Colonel.

'But——'

'Well, is it or isn't it?'

'Yes, but – I can't understand it. It wasn't here. I know it wasn't.'

'It must have been,' said Colonel Wharton, sharply.

Tom scratched his head. 'I don't understand it,' he said again, a puzzled look on his face.

John looked relieved. 'I told you so,' he said, a little note of triumph in his voice.

Colonel Wharton turned to the boy. 'It seems that Mr Wells made a mistake, lad,' he said.

'I'm sorry, John,' muttered Wells.

'Cut along and get on with your work, John.' As he left the room, the Colonel said, 'Well, there you are, Tom. I'm inclined to think that you'd already made up your mind that he would be after it, and so you merely glanced in.'

Wells followed the Colonel out of the room, but at the door he turned round once more, stared at the cake, and shook his head in disbelief.

Billy Bunter let out a snigger. He waited for only a few minutes and then, since it did seem safe at last, he tiptoed into the sitting room, picked up the cake, and cautiously opened the door. The coast was clear. He scuttled along the corridor, and hurried upstairs with his trophy.

This was a prize that he felt he really deserved. He had been prepared to make the supreme sacrifice, and now his virtue had been rewarded. John was in the clear, and the Famous Five would never know what they had missed.

It was fortunate that no one ever went near the dusty, disused attic. If they had, they would have been puzzled by the unexpected sounds coming from it. First they would have heard loud munching noises, and then a long, low rumble, interrupted occasionally by spasmodic snorts as the fat Owl, comfortably wrapped in Harry's blankets and quilt, caught up with his beauty sleep.

CHAPTER 18
A Rift Among Friends

Harry Wharton, standing in the porch of Wharton Lodge, turned round. 'Come on, Bob,' he said cheerfully, but Bob, who was still standing inside the hall, didn't move. 'Shuffle the old feet.'

'Oh, all right,' replied Bob Cherry, and slouched outside. Bob was usually beaming and full of high spirits, but his face was gloomy that afternoon.

Frank whispered to Harry, 'Our Bob's lost his bounce.'

'I know. I expect he'll cheer up later.'

Hurree Singh looked rather concerned as Bob reluctantly joined them, but Johnny Bull only gave a faint grunt as they set off down the drive.

They were on their way to Wimford to see the local pantomime, but judging by the expression on Bob's face, the antics of Widow Twankey had lost their appeal.

They all knew what the matter was. Bob was still brooding over the wrecking of Harry's room last night. He had been hurt because everyone had assumed that he had been guilty, and although he knew that Hurree, Frank and Harry now believed him, he also knew that Johnny did not, and it rankled.

Normally, they would have raced down the drive, but this time they trudged along. They reached the gates of Wharton Lodge in silence, and turned into the main road. Several times Harry tried to start a conversation but each time it petered out. Bob's gloom was catching. Johnny glanced more than once in Bob's direction as if he would like to speak, but the grim look on Bob's face put him off. However, as the lights of Wimford glimmered through the early December dusk, he said at last, 'Look here, Bob,' but Bob just walked a little faster. 'Bob,' Johnny began again, but still there was no response. Johnny caught him up. 'I'm trying to speak to you, Bob Cherry.'

'Don't bother.'

Frank trotted after him. 'I must say I'm looking forward to the panto,' he said, eager to prevent a row. 'I wonder how they managed to get a professional company to come to Wimford. They've always had an amateur show up to now, haven't they?'

Bob and Johnny ignored him. Johnny turned to Bob. 'Don't be such a stupid clot, Bob. What's the good of sulking like this?'

Bob's face reddened. 'Who's sulking?' he snapped.

'You are, nitwit,' said Johnny Bull. 'You've hardly said a word all day. I know that Colonel Wharton didn't say anything about it, but he knew that something was up. Why don't you give it a rest. It's no good walking around with a chip on your shoulder.'

'No?'

'No. I know what you're thinking, Bob. Look what happened last night. So you went a bit too far – so what? It's over. Finished. Forget it.'

Bob shot an angry look at him. 'I couldn't have gone too far since I didn't do anything.'

Johnny gave an exasperated snort. 'What's the point of denying it? If you didn't, who did?'

Bob flashed a suspicious glance at him. 'What about you?'

'Me?' Johnny's face went red.

'That's right. You. It's funny the way you're so keen to put the blame on me. Maybe you know more about it than you've let on.'

'You – you,' spluttered Johnny, almost speechless with rage. 'You rotten, suspicious——'

Harry Wharton hurried up, and elbowed his way between them. 'Shut up, both of you,' he said, quickly. 'Drop it. There's no point in dragging it up again.'

Johnny Bull, breathing hard, threw a furious glance at Bob and marched on ahead.

Harry gripped Bob's elbow. 'Press on, old man.'

Bob shook off his hand and scraped the toe of his shoe in

the snow. 'I'm not coming——'

'What?'

'You heard, Harry. I'm not coming with you. You lot clear off and leave me alone. I've had enough of Johnny. I'll smack his head if I have to listen to him.'

Hurree sighed. 'But perhaps we can arrange things so that you won't have to listen to him. You can sit at one end of the row and he can sit at the other.'

'It wouldn't make any difference. He's made up his mind that I've wrecked Harry's room, and nothing will shake him. No, I'm going to keep out of his way. I'll lose my temper and thump him if he looks at me like that again. I'll go for a walk instead. You go on and——'

'But Bob –' began Harry.

'It's no good,' said Bob, firmly. 'I don't want to have a row with him while we're staying in your uncle's house, so the best thing that I can do is to push off on my own.'

'Oh, jiminy!' groaned Harry. 'Can't you get it into your thick head that I don't even care who did it?'

Bob nodded. 'I know you don't, but it matters to me.'

'Bob, let's screw the lid on the can, and forget all about it.'

'Johnny won't let me forget,' Bob said, stubbornly.

'You're being as pig-headed as he is,' Frank pointed out.

'Too bad.' Bob swung round. 'I hope you enjoy the show,' he said.

Hurree, Frank and Harry watched him marching resolutely away.

'What a rotten show,' said Harry.

'Let's hope that it won't be,' said Hurree, a little smile on his lips. 'We should push on, chaps. It is clear that our friend has made up his mind.'

As they walked on, Frank said, 'They're just a couple of blockheads. Johnny's really got Bob's back up.'

'I know,' agreed Harry. 'When Johnny's got an idea in his head, nothing will shift it – not even an earthquake. He has to be proved wrong first.'

'And there is no way of proving him wrong, is there?' asked Hurree.

'I can't think of one,' said Harry. 'It's just a mystery. I only hope that they both come back in a better mood this evening. It'll ruin the holiday if they don't.

Frank glanced at his watch and broke into a trot. 'Time's getting on,' he said. 'We'll be late.'

Johnny Bull, still stalking ahead, stopped as he heard the sound of running footsteps. 'Where's that fathead Cherry?' he asked.

'He's gone off for a walk,' said Harry, shortly.

Johnny grunted. 'Best thing,' he said. 'I'd have thumped him if I'd had to put up with any more of those suspicious looks. Why he can't admit——'

'Dry up, Johnny,' said Frank, sharply.

They entered the theatre in silence and found their places, miserably aware of the empty seat at the end of the row.

CHAPTER 19

A Brief Encounter

Billy Bunter had spent the morning and most of the afternoon happily tucked up in his dusty attic. Most people would have been a bit depressed at being cooped up, but it hadn't bothered him at all.

The fat Owl was not without his resources, and he had put one of them to good use for most of the day. He was such a master of the art of sleeping that he made Rip van Winkle look like an amateur. He had wrapped himself up and closed his eyes, and then he had snored and grunted his way through hour after hour. Had it not been for his personal alarm clock, he would probably have gone on sleeping.

However, his stomach had rung the warning bell, and so he was huddled in his bed with the quilt wrapped around his shoulders, busily eating the crumbs in his pockets. Unfortunately, they didn't last very long, and so he sat there, his eyes fixed on the window, trying to guess the time. It wasn't the actual hour of the day that interested him – it was whether it was time for lunch or tea or dinner that was important.

Suddenly, his ears twitched, and he turned his eyes anxiously from the window to the door. He was sure that he had heard a very faint footstep, so faint that it might just have been the creaking of the stairs.

Fearfully, he sat still. The stairs creaked again, and his eyes goggled. There was no doubt about it. Someone was ascending those winding attic stairs, someone with a very light tread. Bunter was too terrified to wonder why the visitor was moving so stealthily. He only knew that discovery would be a disaster.

There was a moment of silence, and cautiously William George slipped from the iron bedstead, tiptoed towards the door, and listened, his ears strained for the slightest sound. He was positive that no one had the slightest idea that he was in the house, so it was bad luck that someone had decided to investigate the attic.

He blinked anxiously around, wondering where he could hide, but the bed was too low for him to wriggle under it, and there was nowhere else. He was also dimly aware that even if he had been able to conceal himself, there was plenty of evidence pointing to his occupation of the attic – the crumpled bedclothes, the mound of apple cores, banana skins, and orange peel, as well as crumbs from the cake and biscuits. 'Oh lor'! Oh, lardy cake!' he groaned.

The footsteps had almost reached the top of the stairs by now, but as they did so, Bunter's expression changed from fear to determination, and his little eyes flashed. Well, if he was discovered, and it looked as if he would be, he would be rooted and booted out, but he wasn't going without doing a bit of booting himself, so to speak.

He grabbed his pillow, stepped back to the side of the door again, and held it above his head. It was his only chance. If he could take his visitor by surprise and thump him hard enough, he might be able to hurtle down those stairs and find some other refuge before being recognized.

The soft step was outside the door by now. Billy Bunter's eyes were riveted on the door handle. As it turned, he held his breath. There was a gentle nudge at the door, and it swung open.

Dim though it was, the Owl could make out the slight, small figure of a man as he stepped in. His cap was pulled low over his head, but narrow rat-like eyes gleamed beneath it. Billy Bunter didn't bother to wonder who he was and why he was there. He only knew that the man represented danger, a danger that had to be eliminated. He put everything he'd got into the blow he hurled at the stranger. There was a tremendous thump as the pillow landed right on top of the man's head. The stranger rocked backwards and forwards, and his legs began to buckle.

'Agh! Strike me pink!' he yelped as he slipped, and then he skidded backwards on to the little landing.

'Oh, crikey!' cried Bunter. He had intended to dodge away down the stairs, but the rat-faced man was in the way, blocking his escape route.

The man scrambled to his hands and knees, shaking his head, a dazed expression on his face, and then he staggered up and darted down the stairs and into the corridor. Billy Bunter was astonished. The man had gone! He was alone again.

'Ginger nuts!' he exclaimed as he stood in the room, the pillow still clutched in his fat paws. It had all happened so quickly that he almost wondered whether he had imagined it. The whole incident was quite extraordinary. He turned the matter over in his head. What on earth did it mean? What could it mean? And then, very slowly, light began to dawn. The man was an outsider. He was nothing to do with Wharton Lodge at all.

'Aha!' he said to himself. 'So that was why he was wearing a cap and a coat.' After all, no one else would be wearing them indoors. No wonder he had taken to his heels and raced off after that surprise attack. Quite clearly he had been as alarmed as the fat Owl himself.

Billy Bunter's sluggish brain began to turn over a little more quickly. He was probably a thief, someone who had slipped in and prowled around, hoping to pick up a few trifles before sneaking out again. The Owl's fat face went pale. He'd tangled with a villain, and swiped him with Harry's pillows. His knees knocked, and his hands shook. Suppose he returned to take his revenge! Beads of perspiration broke out on his brow. He might come back!

He sank back on to the bed in despair, but the despair disappeared as he found himself sitting on an old apple that he had unaccountably overlooked. He sat chewing, and as he chewed, his optimism returned. The thief had probably been just as frightened of him. After all, he couldn't have known that the Owl himself was an intruder. He would have thought that he was a guest, and he would have expected him to raise the alarm. He would have put as much distance between himself and Wharton Lodge as he could.

No, Bunter decided. He was safe. He was still quite secure in his hideout. There was no need to panic, and so the Owl munched on.

CHAPTER 20
An Old Acquaintance

At the very moment that Billy Bunter was listening to the tread of quiet footsteps approaching the attic door, Bob Cherry was coming across the lawn towards the fight of steps that led up to Harry's quarters, a disgruntled look on his face.

As he had said he would, he had been for a long tramp, but as the light had faded, he had made his way back to Wharton Lodge. He was still feeling depressed. The last thing that he wanted to do was to cast a shadow over the Christmas festivities, and he certainly didn't want Colonel or Mrs Wharton to suspect that anything was wrong, but he was still upset.

And so he gave a loud sigh as he climbed the stone steps to the balcony. By going in that way, no one else in the house need know that the party had split up and that he'd gone off on his own. Once inside, he could settle down with a book and only put in an appearance when the others came back from the pantomime.

He was about to push the door open when he remembered they had decided to keep it locked. 'Bother!' he said and stood there, a glum expression on his face. He'd either have to hang around in the cold until the rest of the Famous Five came home or he would have to ring the door bell, and then they'd find out that he'd mooched off on his own. Bother that rotten old tramp or whoever it was who had got in the othe day!

Annoyed, he kicked the door. There was a slight creak, and it swung open. 'Oh, my Sunday titfer!' exclaimed Bob, surprised that it hadn't been locked. Well, it was a stroke of luck for him.

The room was dim, with only the embers of the log fire glowing faintly in the fireplace, lights and shadows dancing on the walls as little tongues of flame flickered up and down. Bob fumbled for the light switch, switched it on, and then threw his anorak and gloves on the settee. He strolled over to the fire, picked up the poker, and stirred it into life before throwing on a few logs. Soon there was a bright and cheerful blaze.

He stood in front of it, thinking about Johnny, and then he gave himself a shake. It was no good brooding. Resolutely, he put his trouble out of his mind, wandered across to the bookcase in the corner of the room, and ran his eyes over the titles. Just as he had picked up a thick novel, he heard a noise, and then the sound of racing footsteps. Someone was coming along the corridor at a fair old lick. Startled, he looked up.

'What the thump!' he said to himself. The door was flung open, and a small man wearing an overcoat and a cap ran into the room. Bob's eyes nearly popped out of his head. He knew that slight figure. He was the man who had broken in the previous day.

The man didn't spot Bob. He checked his headlong flight, blinked as if surprised by the light in the room, and made for the french windows. It was so unexpected that Bob didn't have a chance of tackling him, but he hurled the heavy book, and it landed with a thud on the side of the man's head. He grunted, staggered, and slid to the ground. Bob pounced, grabbing the slight figure and pinning him down.

'Help!' he bellowed at the top of his voice. 'Help!'

The rat-faced man turned on him like a trapped animal,

twisting and turning violently, trying to break free. Small though he was, he was strong and wiry, and as slippery as an eel. He struggled savagely, using every ounce of his strength as Bob clung on.

'Help! Colonel Wharton! Wells! Bob heard people pounding along the corridor.

'What's going on?' called Colonel Wharton.

'Quick! I've got him!' roared Bob.

The door was thrown open, and Colonel Wharton appeared in the doorway, with Tom Wells and John at his heels. The man made one last desperate effort. He kicked hard, and as Bob's grip loosened, he tore himself free. He was on his feet in a flash, facing the Colonel.

There was a cry from Tom Wells. 'It's him again!'

Colonel Wharton stared, his bushy eyebrows raised. 'You – you villain!' he cried, astonished.

As they stood there, the man saw his chance and raced towards the balcony.

'I'll – I'll – You wait till I get my hands on you!' shouted the Colonel, as he rushed after him.

Bob struggled up, breathless from his struggle. 'Who is he?'

Tom and John charged after the Colonel. 'It's the burglar!' Tom said.

'Golly!' Bob pulled himself together, and scrambled up, and then he too raced out. He skidded to a halt at the foot of the steps. It was so dark by now that he could see nothing but the glimmer of the snow. There was the sound of heavy breathing, and then Colonel Wharton, Wells and John appeared.

'He got away then?' asked Bob.

Colonel Wharton frowned. 'Yes,' he said, shortly, and led the way back into Harry's sitting room.

'Was he really the chap who stole your Tintoretto?'

'No doubt about it,' said the Colonel, gruffly.

'It was him, all right,' said Tom Wells. 'I'd know him anywhere.'

Colonel Wharton stroked his moustache. 'And to think we had him within our grasp!' he said, ruefully. 'The effrontery of the man! He must have picked the lock of this door. I'll have to get a bolt fixed.'

'I must say he's got plenty of nerve, coming back like this,' said Bob.

'I wonder what he came for?' said the Colonel. 'I'd better ring the police straight away. The rest of you have a look round, will you? See if anything's missing.'

'He's a right villain!' Tom Wells said over and over again to Bob as they searched.

It was some time before Colonel Wharton returned. 'There's nothing missing downstairs,' he said. 'What about up here?'

'No,' said Tom Wells, positively. 'It's all here. Nothing's been disturbed.'

'Perhaps he'd only just got here,' suggested Bob.

'Well, what happened, m'boy?'

'I don't know,' confessed Bob. 'All I heard was a noise in the corridor, and then he shot in here like a bullet from a gun.'

'He couldn't have been here for long since nothing's missing. I suppose something disturbed him. Now, what could it be?' The Colonel turned to Tom Wells. 'Where were you?'

'I was in the kitchen with cook.'

'And you, John?'

'I was helping Mr Wells with the silver.'

'That's right,' agreed Tom. 'He was under mv eyes all of the time. Alice wasn't in. It's her afternoon off.'

Puzzled, the Colonel shook his head. 'It's quite extraordinary. What could have frightened him off?' he asked, but no one could come up with any ideas.

The fact was, Colonel Wharton was asking the wrong people. There was someone who could have enlightened him, but that someone was upstairs, and sleeping soundly.

CHAPTER 21

Late Hours

That someone lifted his head from his pillow later that evening. 'Oh, lor'!' he mumbled.

Yawning, he sat up on the bedstead, hugging his blankets

tightly, and mumbled 'Oh, lor'!' again. He had stuffed himself with biscuits and cake that morning, and more biscuits and an apple later on, and these had temporarily filled his aching void, but now he was conscious that he was ravenous again.

He gnawed his lower lip. He still couldn't reveal himself. The miracle he had so confidently expected hadn't taken place. He had hoped that by now he would have been able to come into the open where he would be welcomed by a genial Colonel Wharton, a rapturous Aunt Amy, and the delighted faces of the Famous Five, and then led to a table groaning with Christmas goodies, but it hadn't happened yet.

Although he was convinced that his chance would come, he couldn't sit around waiting. After all, a fellow had to eat. He simply had to have some grub, whatever the risk. He'd rather take the chance of a booting and Bunter Villa than put up with the pangs of hunger for much longer.

So he sat there, making his plans. All he had to do was wait patiently until the household went to bed, and then he could creep downstairs. He knew where the kitchen was, he knew where the fridge was, and he knew where the larder was. It was just a matter of time.

He wrapped himself up once more, and tried to go to sleep. Usually he dropped off straight away, but it was no good this time. The ache in his stomach kept him awake. He blinked dismally in the darkness, wondering what the time was. It looked as if it was late, and it felt late, but was it? Was it safe for a hungry Owl to patter down those stairs?

Well, there was only one way to find out. He clambered off the bed, fumbled for the door handle, and went down the stairs.

'Beasts!' he said, as he peered into the corridor. The lights were on, so they must still be up. He'd have to wait a bit longer. Gloomily, he sat on the stairs, and put his chin in his hands. 'Beasts!'

A few minutes later, he brightened up. Maybe the Famous Five had gone to bed, and only Colonel and Mrs Wharton were up. If that was so, it might be safe for him to creep into Wharton's sitting room and see if there was any grub going. Aunt Amy might well have sent fresh supplies up. It was risky.

. . . he was conscious that he was ravenous again.

There was always a chance that if the Famous Five were in bed, they might still be awake. Still, he had to take the chance. His stomach wouldn't let him rest.

Quickly, he made his way down once again, and blinked first one way, and then the other. All the doors were closed. He put one fat toe down on to the corridor, and stood thinking and blinking. Ten to one that gang were fast asleep, but suppose they were still downstairs? Suppose they caught him? He shuddered at the thought, but a warning rumble from his stomach made him go on. He had to have food.

He slipped on toward his goal. He stopped in frozen horror as he heard a sound coming from a bedroom, but then he breathed again. It was only someone turning over in bed.

Reassured, he crept on until he reached Harry's room, and he bent a fat ear to the door, his hand already on the handle, and then he let go as if it were red hot. Bob Cherry was speaking.

'It's no good.'

'Look here, Bob.' Wharton sounded worried. 'Why——?'

'It's no good. I'd better go to bed. It's getting late. Frank and Hurree will be asleep by now, and blockhead Bull will be snoring his head off.'

'Ah!' thought Bunter. So only two of the crowd were up. That was something, but it wasn't enough. He shook his clenched fist at the door. Why couldn't they go to bed as well, and leave him to forage in peace?'

'No, don't go yet, Bob.'

'It's no good yammering on like this,' said Bob, in a depressed voice. 'We can't go on like this. Johnny and I are at loggerheads. My hands have been itching to thump that stubborn idiot. I would have done if I hadn't been staying here.'

'There's no need for you to be at loggerheads,' said Harry, reasonably.

'Isn't there?' snapped Bob. 'He's got it into his head that I shipped your bed. You know Johnny. Once he's got an idea stuck in his thick head, nothing will change it.'

'I know that all right,' said Harry, wearily, 'but——'

'He won't take my word, will he?'

101

'It's not exactly that. He would believe you, but he thinks it's all part of the leg pull. You can see why——'

Bob's voice rose. 'It sounds as if you're on his side.'

'Don't be so idiotic, Bob!'

There was silence, and then Bob spoke again. 'It's stupid, Harry,' he said, miserably, 'but there doesn't seem to be any way to patch it up. I'm sorry, but I've made up my mind. I'm going to clear off in the morning.'

'Bob!' Harry was dismayed. 'You can't! It wouldn't be the same without you!'

'It isn't the same now. No, I honestly think——'

'Don't. We'll get to the bottom of it sooner or later. Something odd is going on. Tom Wells told me a queer story this evening. A cake was put in this room this morning, but when he came up, it had disappeared. Then, when my uncle came up to investigate, there it was.'

'Perhaps Tom made a mistake.'

'I don't think so. Tom wouldn't go blaming John for its disappearance unless it really had gone. But the queerest thing about it is that the cake vanished again. We didn't see it, did we?'

'No.'

'So where did it go?' At this, Billy Bunter clapped his fat hand to his mouth to smother his sniggers. 'Look, Bob,' Harry went on. 'We'll sort it out before long, and then Johnny will be convinced——'

'I don't care whether that blithering clot is convinced or not!' Bob burst out. 'I'm fed up with him, and I'm fed up with his suspicious mind. We can't go on like this, not even speaking to each other. You uncle knows that something is up, and your aunt will soon cotton on. I don't want to spoil their Christmas too. I shall clear out in the morning.'

'You can't!'

'I can, and I will. I've made up my mind, Harry, and you can't change it. Let's go to bed.'

'Not until we've settled this,' said Harry, firmly.

'We've settled it – at least, I have.'

'But I haven't. Bob, can't I get you to change——?'

'No you can't. It's hopeless. One of us has got to go, and I think it should be me.'

'Bob!'

'I'm going to bed.' As Bob's heavy footsteps trampled towards the door, Bunter fled, well aware that there wasn't time for him to reach the attic stairs. As he reached a door, he skidded to a halt, swiftly turned the knob, and slipped in. He hadn't any idea of whose room it was, but he didn't care. Nothing mattered as long as he was out of sight. He stood with his back to the door, his ears strained to catch the slightest sound.

'Don't be so daft,' Harry Wharton said. He must have followed Bob into the corridor.

'Good night,' said Bob, briefly.

'I'm not going to bed. I'm coming with you.'

A door opened, and Harry and Bob continued talking in the corridor. Bunter sighed. He'd have to wait until they went into Bob's room.

There was a sound from the far side of the room.

'Who's that?' asked Johnny.

Johnny hadn't been properly asleep. He'd dozed off, but it had been an uneasy doze. Like Bob, he was aware of how absurd the situation was. They could hardly go on not speaking to each other without other people noticing, but he couldn't see how to get out of it. He was convinced that Bob was playing some complicated game of his own, and that that was why he wouldn't come clean.

There was nothing complicated about Johnny Bull. He himself was a straightforward person, and so he couldn't imagine what the game was or why Bob was playing it, but he was sure that there was one. He just wanted Bob to admit that he had been playing the giddy goat so that they could forget about it, and get down to enjoying the Christmas hols. So he lay in bed, half asleep, only to be jerked awake as he heard heavy breathing inside the room.

'Who's that?' he demanded again, sitting upright, and peering into the darkness. 'It's you, isn't it, Bob Cherry? What are you up to?' There was silence. 'Speak up, you fathead!'

Billy Bunter kept his mouth firmly closed, and stood trembling by the door, fearful that Johnny might switch the light on.

'You clown! I know it's you, you dithering dummy! You must think me a fool, Cherry! Going to play the same trick on me, were you? I'll show you whether I'm a fool or not!'

A pillow whizzed through the air. As it landed on Billy Bunter's chest, and thudded to the floor, he let out an anguished yelp.

'I'll get you!' roared Johnny, and he scrambled out of bed.

At the very same moment there was a noise which sounded like music in Billy Bunter's ear. It was a click as Bob's door was closed. The coast was clear! He could scuttle up the corridor again, but he wasn't quite out of the woods. Johnny was on the warpath.

No one could claim that the fat Owl was much of an athlete, but now, in this moment of danger, he behaved like one. As a stocky figure came towards him, he grasped the pillow, and hurled it. There was a thump as it hit its target, and Johnny fell heavily on to the floor.

Billy Bunter didn't wait to enjoy his triumph. He was outside the door in a flash, banging it shut, and then raced up to the attic at such a rate that his plump little feet hardly seemed to touch the ground.

CHAPTER 22
Not Bob!

'Oh! Urrrgh!' gasped Johnny Bull, sitting up dizzily, and rubbing his sore head. 'Oh, crumbs!' By gum, I – I – I'll——'

It was some moments before he got to his feet. That sudden blow had been a bit of a shock. He knew that he was alone in the room, but he jolly well knew where to look for his assailant.

Breathing hard, he switched on the light, dragged on his dressing gown, and stomped out into the corridor. With a grim

104

face, he marched down to Bob Cherry's room. There wasn't anybody about, but then, he didn't expect to see anyone. Bob would have scuttled back to the safety of his room by now.

Johnny reached the door. He flung it open without bothering to knock, and stormed in. 'You stupid twit!' he roared. 'Who do you think you are? You must think I'm a mug, barging into my room like that! I'm going to teach you a lesson, Cherry!'

Bob Cherry, still fully dressed, was sitting on the edge of his bed, and he looked up blankly as Johnny charged in like an enraged bull. He was far too surprised to say anything, and Harry, standing by the fireplace, was equally astonished.

Johnny shook his fist at Bob. 'What were you going to do, that's what I'd like to know,' he shouted, furiously. 'Thought you could ship my bed, did you, but with me in it? You blithering ass, you stupid dithering dunderhead——'

Bob spoke at last. 'Mad?' he asked.

'By gum!' grasped Johnny. 'Are you going to say you weren't in my room, Bob Cherry? Are you saying you didn't floor me with my own pillow? Is that it?'

'What – what do you mean? Are you saying that somebody was prowling round your room?'

'That's right. You were, and I'm jolly well going to punch your thick head in!' shouted Johnny, making a rush for Bob.

Harry moved quickly. He grabbed hold of Johnny Bull's collar, and yanked him back. Johnny spun round, and his jaw dropped as he saw Harry.

'You mad ass!' exclaimed Harry Wharton. 'What the dickens do you think——?'

'Take your hands off me!' snapped Johnny.

'What's this all about?' demanded Harry.

'I thought you'd gone to bed.'

'I had!' shouted Johnny.

'I was half asleep when that loopy lunatic came in. I'm going to punch his silly head! You can let him wreck your room and get away with it if you like, but he's not going to do the same to me, and thump me with my own pillow into the bargain.'

'Potty,' said Bob. 'He's gone round the twist. Lost his marbles.'

'You——'

'Shut up, Johnny, and listen,' said Harry. 'Bob didn't do it. Are you sure you didn't imagine it?'

'Imagine it!' hooted Johnny. 'I ought to have known whether I was floored or not. That loony over there——'

'Somebody really was in your room then?'

'I've just told you, and I know who it was. It was that blistering ass——'

'When?' asked Harry, sharply.

'A couple of minutes ago.'

'Then it couldn't have been Bob.'

'If it wasn't him, then who was it?'

'I don't know, but it wasn't Bob. He's been with me ever since we came upstairs. He hasn't been out of my sight. First of all we were in my room, and then we came in here.'

Flabbergasted, Johnny turned from one to the other, and then he looked back at Harry. 'Honestly?'

'Honestly.'

'I – I – well, I was sure it was Bob larking about again. What else was I to think?'

'What else?' said Bob, sarcastically. 'And now you know it wasn't me, who are you going to blame now? Frank, maybe, or Hurree.'

'I – I – I thought' stammered Johnny.

'You did what? That's a change, isn't it?'

'As soon as I heard someone, I chucked my pillow, and then I got out of bed, but he whacked me with it, and as I went down I cracked my head and——'

'Hard, I hope,' said Bob, unsympathetically.

'But if – if – if it wasn't you – but in that case, who——'

'Why not go and pick a quarrel with the others?' suggested Bob. 'Actually, I don't care what you do as long as you get out of here.'

'It wouldn't have been either of them,' said Harry.

'What wouldn't?' Two figures stood in the doorway, one with a blazer over his pyjamas, the other wearing a gorgeous dressing gown.

'Have we woken you up?' asked Harry.

'I don't want to complain, my dear Harry, but the noise

coming from this room would have awoken the dead.'

'You'd better watch out,' said Bob. 'Johnny's on the warpath. Somebody's been larking about in his room and he's going to punch someone's head, and it doesn't matter whose it is.'

'I – er – I thought –' mumbled Johnny. He hardly knew what to think. 'I – I know it wasn't you, Hurree, and it couldn't be Frank, so I thought it was Bob, but now – well, it wasn't him either.'

'Hark at Brain of Britain,' said Bob, mockingly. 'Now that he's got that into his thick head perhaps he'll admit that I might have been telling the truth when I said I wasn't in Harry's room.'

'There has to be a practical joker around,' said Frank Nugent. 'It was Harry's room last night, and now it's Johnny's. Somebody's playing the giddy goat.'

'That's true,' said Harry. 'Somebody's been playing tricks, and we know for sure that it wasn't one of us.'

'But does Johnny know that?' asked Bob.

Johnny's face went crimson. He was slow to give up an idea once it was fixed firmly in his head, but he knew now that he was completely and hopelessly wrong.

'Well, do you?' asked Bob.

Johnny gulped. 'Sorry,' he said, at last.

'I should jolly well think so,' said Bob.

'I admit that I was wrong, Bob, but honestly I couldn't help thinking that——'

'You didn't think at all.'

'But it did look fishy.'

'It only looked fishy to a silly, obstinate ass.'

'Look,' said Johnny, 'I've said I'm sorry.'

'I heard you, and now you've got round to it, you can get out and let me get to bed.'

Johnny Bull turned to the door. The others looked at Bob's set face, and exchanged troubled glances. It seemed that nothing had changed. Johnny put his hand on the door handle, and then he turned back. 'Look here, Bob,' he said. 'I was wrong, and I've said so. I'm sorry, and I've said it more than once. Let's bury the hatchet. It's not like you to hold a grudge. Can't we forget about it?'

Bob Cherry's grim expression disappeared, and a grin spread across his face. 'Okay,' he said. 'Let's, but just wait for tomorrow. It'll be our turn to go on the warpath. We'll get that practical joker, whoever he is, and then we'll skin him alive.'

'You bet!' said Frank Nugent, enthusiastically.

'It is getting chilly,' said Harry Wharton. 'We'd better all turn in. Goodnight, you chaps.'

There was a chorus of goodnights, and they made their way to their rooms, relieved that the misunderstandings were over, and determined to catch the culprit on the following day. They had no idea that they wouldn't have to wait that long.

CHAPTER 23

Awful for Bunter!

'Oh, golly!' gasped Billy Bunter. He was afraid that he would hear feet pounding up the stairs after him, but there were none. Instead, doors banged, and then he heard the faint murmur of voices.

At last, he sank on to his bed, and wrapped the bedclothes round himself. He was tired, but he knew that he couldn't possibly go to sleep. He still hadn't managed to supply his capacious stomach with food, and it knew it. It wasn't going to let him rest, but he would have to live with those dreadful pangs of hunger until the whole household was asleep.

The time crawled past. Every minute seemed like an hour to the hungry Owl. He stirred restlessly, wondering just how long he had been waiting. Although he wasn't quite sure what a century was, he didn't think it had been quite as long as that. He decided to leave it a little longer. That stuffy old stick Colonel Wharton might still be up. He was only consoled by the thought that the larder was bound to be crammed with delicious food.

There was a sudden unexpected creak. Billy Bunter started up, and he drew the blankets higher up to his chin. 'Oh, crikey!' he said, nervously, as he heard the noise again. His eyes and spectacles swivelled round to the attic door. That creak, coming as it did in the middle of the night, was alarming. Were those beasts on his track at last?

Creak! There it was again. His fat heart gave another jump. No, he thought. It couldn't be them. They wouldn't creep quietly up the stairs, but he knew who would – that sneak thief, the man with the glittering rat-like eyes, the intruder who had fled in wild haste.

Billy Bunter bit his lip. 'Oh, humbugs!' He'd swiped the man with his pillow, hadn't he? He'd prided himself on routing the fellow, but now he trembled with fear. Perhaps he was coming back to do a bit of swiping himself.

There was another sudden creak, but this time Bunter merely looked puzzled. He had been listening hard, and he was sure that the noise hadn't come from the direction of the door at all. It wasn't the sound of a footstep. Nobody was creeping up that winding staircase.

Then what was it? He stretched his ears, and waited for the noise again. Creak! There it was. Billy Bunter almost laughed. He knew what it was now. It came from the little attic window.

He sighed with relief. The window was old. No wonder it gave out that dismal sound whenever the wind blew. Probably the old iron drain pipe that ran up alongside it creaked in sympathy too.

Reassured, he hugged his blankets round him, and then gave a sudden start. No wonder he was cold. There was a chilly draught of air coming from the window. It took some time for the significance of this to penetrate his sluggish mind, and then he goggled. The window was open!

He blinked in alarm. The room was pitch dark and only a glimmer of light came through the panes, but as he watched, that light was blotted out by something solid. The Owl trembled with fear as he realized that he was looking at a man who was clambering into the room. He sat where he was, crouched in his corner and petrified by fear, his eyes bulging as a slight figure dropped lightly to the floor. It was the intruder again!

There was a click. Light flickered in the dark room. The man was holding a torch. Billy Bunter held his breath and crossed his fingers, hoping that it wouldn't be turned in his direction.

It wasn't. The man concentrated the light on the door, and stepped across to it. Silently, he opened it, and listened intently. Satisfied, he moved to an old box and placed the torch on it so that the light streamed on to the floor. He dropped to his knees, knelt by the side of the dusty square of carpet, and carefully turned back one edge.

He gave a low, husky chuckle. 'Ha! Safe and sound, just as I thought it would be. Fools, that's what they are! Fools! As if I could have got down the drain pipe with it! They must be thick.'

Billy Bunter was completely baffled. The man might have been talking Greek as far as he was concerned, but at least he realized that there was something hidden underneath that shabby old carpet – something that had to be important otherwise he wouldn't have risked his neck by climbing up a shaky old drain pipe.

Frozen with terror, the Owl kept his eyes fixed on that square of carpet. There was another throaty laugh. 'Third time lucky. Thought I'd never manage to get my hands on it again.' He kneeled back, and shot a glance at the window. 'Well, I can't get down that way. Still, there's nothing to stop me going out of the front door. Bolts and bars keep thieves out, but they don't keep them in.' He bent down again. 'Come along, my beauty. Let's have a gander!'

As he chuckled, the man folded back more of the carpet, and the light from the torch streamed on to the floorboards, but it streamed on to something else as well. There was a glow of rich colours as the light rested on a marvellous painting.

Billy Bunter almost wondered if he was dreaming. There he was, sitting in a disused attic, looking at a canvas brilliant with colour – a canvas that had been covered by a carpet. What the fat Owl didn't know about art would have filled a book – lots and lots of books, in fact – but he did know a picture when he saw one, and this was stunning. He drew in his breath.

The man's sharp ears must have caught the faint sound. He turned his head, and his eyes swept around the dark attic.

Rapidly, he dropped the carpet back over the painting and jumped up, grabbed the torch, and swept a beam of light over the room in a circle. It flashed into the alcove on one side of the fireplace, and then it flashed into the other.

Billy Bunter was caught in that beam of light. He sat there, an expression of terror on his face, his blankets clutched around him.

The man made no movement. He stood there, the torch in one hand, a look of utter astonishment on his face, and as he stared at Bunter, Bunter stared back like a rabbit hypnotized by a snake. The man made a slight movement, and the spell was broken.

With a howl of terror, the fat Owl bounded from the bedstead. Hardly knowing what he was doing, he hurled the blankets at the man, and bolted for the door. Enveloped in the whirling blankets, the man lost his balance, spun round, and collided with the end of the bed. As he crashed down, he dropped the torch, and the light went out.

Billy Bunter reached the door. He grabbed the handle and yanked it open. 'Help! Help! Burglars!' he yelled, at the top of his voice. 'Help! Thieves!'

His frantic cries echoed up and down the corridor below, and there was a babble of noise as fellows hurtled out of their bedrooms. The Owl charged for the landing, but he missed his target and crashed into the doorpost. There was another ear-splitting yell as his fat little nose was flattened. 'Yarooo!' Stumbling about in the dark, the Owl tottered backwards and fell on to the carpet, rolling over and over on the blankets that the thief had torn from himself.

'Hallo, hallo, hallo!'

'What's up?'

'What the thump——?'

'Who's that?'

'Where's that noise coming from?'

The Famous Five milled about at the bottom of the stairs, and their voices floated up to the attic, but Bunter didn't hear them. His fat ears were filled by his own musical efforts as he yelled and yelled, afraid of the punishment the rat-faced man might hand out.

Billy Bunter was caught in that beam of light.

What he didn't know was that he was alone in the attic. The burglar, as terrified as the Owl himself, had fled. He scrambled out of the tiny window, and had slipped and slithered down the drain pipe, anxious to get away while the going was good.

He only just made it. Lights were switched on, and racing footsteps thundered up the attic stairs, but Billy Bunter was unaware of all this. He only knew that he was scared out of his fat wits, and so he lay sprawled on the dusty carpet, and went on yelling.

CHAPTER 24

Only Bunter!

'It's Bunter!' exclaimed Harry, shining his torch into the attic.
'Who?'

'Did you say that it is our fat friend?' asked Hurree Singh.

'That's right.' Harry moved to one side, and held the torch high so that the crowd on the small landing could see for themselves.

'But how on earth——?'

'What's he doing here?'

'It really is Bunter the Lionheart,' said Hurree, smiling at the fat figure which was rolling round and round, yelling at the top of its voice.

Bunter went on threshing about. 'Help! Help! Thieves! I – I say, you fellows! Keep off! – Leggo!' He fought wildly with the blankets that were draped over him. 'Oh, crikey! Beast! Help! Help!'

They watched him tussling with his enemy, smiling, but completely bewildered. They couldn't imagine why he was yelling for help. They couldn't imagine why he was there. He was alone in the attic. There wasn't a burglar in sight. The whole thing was a mystery.

Bunter went on threshing about.

'What's that fat villain doing here?' demanded Johnny.

'It is him. It's not his ghost, is it?' asked Frank.

Hurree Singh gave a quiet laugh. 'I think not, my dear Frank. That mound of flesh looks quite solid to me.'

'But how did he get here in the middle of the night?' asked Bob.

'Dashed if I know,' replied Harry.

Billy Bunter's fat legs flailed around. There were more bellows from beneath the blankets. 'Help! I – I say – Help! Burglars!'

'Bunter, you ridiculous rhino –' As Frank bent down to help him out of the tangle of blankets, Bunter kicked out. 'Ouch, you ass!' he cried.

'Keep off! Leggo! Help!'

Bob stooped down, and ripped the blankets away. 'Shut up!' he shouted. 'You'll wake the whole house up, you fat fraud!'

'Oh!' gasped the Owl.

For the first time he seemed to realize that the danger was over. He sat up on the old, faded carpet, and blinked up at the juniors who were crowding round him. Then he shuddered, flashing an uneasy glance round the room. 'I – I – I say, you fellows. Where – where is he? Where's he gone?'

'What are you on about?' demanded Bob, impatiently.

Bunter gave another nervous blink around the attic. 'Him!' he said, anxiously.

'Who?'

'The burglar – the burglar!'

'What are you talking about, fathead?'

'It – it was a burglar. I – I say, has he gone? He – he jolly nearly had me. Honestly, it was one. Give your uncle a shout, Wharton. Tell Wells. Tell everyone. Call the police.'

'Not likely,' said Harry. 'Listen to me, you fat chump. When we got here, you were alone.'

'But it was!' yelled Bunter, indignantly. 'I tell you it was! I should know, shouldn't I? It – it was a burglar.'

'And what was he pinching? That old bedstead, or these boxes, you fat lunatic, or maybe he was after the washstand.'

'But——'

'Stop burbling. What I want to know is what you're doing here?'

'And how did you get here?' asked Bob. 'What's your game, you fat, footling, frumptious freak?'

'I – I – I – I say, you fellows,' stuttered Bunter. 'Just – just look around. He – he could still be hiding. Look under the bed, will you, Hurree, old man?'

'I assure you, my dear Bunter, that no one could squeeze under that bed.'

As Hurree pointed, they all looked at the crumpled bed and the mound of rubbish that Billy Bunter had deposited on the floor.

Bob stared. 'Look!' he exclaimed. 'Look at that, Harry. That's where your bedding went.'

'What!' Harry turned on Bunter. 'You – you pilfering poacher! You pinched my bedding. You – you——'

As he advanced on the Owl, Bunter cowered. 'I – I – wasn't me! Didn't do nothing. Tain't fair. I – I wouldn't ship your bed, old man. Wouldn't dream of it. Anyway, ain't the way to treat a guest——'

'A guest!' roared Harry. 'And who invited you, you loathsome leech?'

'But – but I knew you really wanted me – only a little misunderstanding, Harry, old chap.'

'How did he get here?' asked Bob.

'Search me. I thought that he was back at home. I tell you, fat man, that I'm going to do just what I said. I'm going to boot you all round the county.'

'Twice!' said Johnny.

'But – but, I say, you chaps——'

'Don't you but me!' said Harry, grimly. 'You shipped my bed, wrecked my room——'

'Pinched your blankets——'

'Who? Me? I – I – I didn't. Wouldn't. Not me.'

'Then how did they get here?'

'I – I dunno – how should I know. Anyway, it's been jolly cold, hasn't it? I mean, you wouldn't want a fellow to freeze to death in your uncle's house, would you? Chap's got to have bedclothes, ain't he?'

'You – you – you——'

'Never touched your bed, Harry, old chap,' gabbled the Owl. 'Must have been some other bloke. Nasty trick. Besides, it was only a joke.'

'You lying rat!' roared Bob.

'What are you doing here anyway?'

'I – er – that is, I – I –' Billy Bunter sat bolt upright on the carpet, and gave the Famous Five an uneasy blink through his big, round specs. His fear of the burglar had gone, but another fear had taken its place. A booting would be bad enough, but to be returned to Bunter Villa would be far worse.

Bob gazed down at Bunter. 'He's been at the bottom of it all,' he said. 'He must have been the bloke in your room, Johnny. He must have whacked you with your pillow.'

'If he'd only get up, I'd floor him,' he said, savagely.

There was a wild yell from Billy Bunter. 'You keep off, Johnny Bull, you beast! I never went in your room. Didn't know where it was. Why should I? Besides, you chucked it at me first, you jolly well know you did. Wasn't doing anything – winded me, that pillow did.'

'Scrag him!' bellowed Johnny.

'Boot him!'

'Bump him!'

'I – I say, chaps, keep off!' howled the Owl. 'I – I – I had to get out of that snow, didn't I? Had to go somewhere. I wasn't really hiding, not really. I was – well, I was just keeping it dark for the moment, I – I wanted to give you a surprise, that's all. I – I knew how much you'd like it, Harry, old man. Course I knew how much you wanted me for Christmas – that's why I was going to give you a surprise.'

Harry Wharton took the torch from Hurree Singh's hands, and lodged it on the mantelpiece. 'Thought you'd like to keep your hands free, Hurree,' he said.

'What – what for?' asked Bunter, anxiously.

'You'll see.' Harry turned to his friends. 'We can hardly boot him out at this time of night, can we?'

'I – I should jolly well think not!' gasped Bunter, indignantly. 'That's not the way to treat a guest!'

'But we can do that tomorrow——'

'Oh, really, Wharton——'

117

'Instead of booting him all round the county, we'll go easy on him, and simply boot him to Wimford, and boot him into a train——'

'Beast!' wailed Billy Bunter.

'But we might as well bump him while we're here.'

'Good idea!' said Johnny Bull, enthusiastically.'Well, let's get on with it!'

'I say, you fellows – leggo! Hands off!' yelled Bunter as the Famous Five grabbed him and swept him up from the floor. 'I say – I wasn't – I didn't – I never – Wow! Ow! Ooooch!'

There was a thunderous bump, and a cloud of dust rose in the air. Billy Bunter opened his mouth wide, and roared. 'Yarooo! Oh, crikey! Gruuump!'

'Give him another!'

'You bet!'

'Ready?'

The fat Owl yelled again in anticipation of the next bump, but at that moment there was a heavy tread on the landing outside the attic. The juniors looked at each other, and let go of the fat Owl.

CHAPTER 25
Startling Discovery!

'What's all this?' demanded Colonel Wharton, as he strode into the attic.

He came to a halt at the unexpected sight of six boys. Five of them were wearing coats or dressing gowns over their pyjamas. The sixth was a fat figure with a dirty face. He was dressed in crumpled clothes, and he lay sprawling on the floor.

'Harry! What is going on? Who is this boy? What's he doing here?'

'It's Bunter.'

'Bunter?'

'Don't you remember, Uncle James. He stayed here——'

'Yes, yes, of course I do.' Colonel Wharton didn't sound

particularly fond of Billy Bunter. 'What the dickens is he doing here? You didn't ask him, did you? I think you had better explain. I cannot imagine what has caused this uproar.'

'Bunter thought that there was a burglar up here. He started yelling, and that woke us up, so we——'

'You weren't the only people to be woken up,' said Colonel Wharton, grimly. 'The whole house is probably awake by now. But you still haven't told me what he is doing here.'

'I think he'd better tell you himself,' said Harry.

'Well?' The Colonel turned to the fat Owl.

Billy Bunter scrambled awkwardly to his feet, set his round specs straight on his fat little nose, and gave Colonel Wharton an uneasy grin.

'Everything all right, Colonel Wharton?' It was Wells who had arrived on the landing.

'I am just about to find out.' The Colonel directed his gaze on to Bunter once more. 'Well? Out with it! What does this mean?'

'Oh! Er – well, nothing,' gasped Bunter.

'How did you get here?'

'I just – just walked in.'

'You walked in?' repeated Colonel Wharton. 'When did you walk in? How did you walk in? Every door and window in this house was securely locked. I checked them myself.'

'Not this evening, Uncle James,' said Harry. 'He barged in some time yesterday——'

'Yesterday?' said the Colonel, incredulously. 'Then where has he been? Why have I not seen him?'

'Up here, I think.'

'Up here! In this attic! Without my knowledge! Is that right, Bunter? Have you been hiding here ever since yesterday?'

'I – I – I – No! I – er – I – that is, yes,' gabbled Billy Bunter. 'You see, I – I – I wasn't quite sure that – that Harry expected me – so that's why——'

'You fat villain!' burst out Harry.

'Oh, really, Wharton, that's not very friendly.'

'Will you kindly get on with your story?' snapped Colonel Wharton.

'There – there was a little misunderstanding when we broke up for the hols,' mumbled Bunter. 'He – he misunderstood something I said – no, something I didn't say when we were still at Greyfriars. Of course, I knew that Harry was really keen for me to come for Christmas – an old pal like me – but we, we sort of got across each other, and somehow he forgot to ask me. I – I knew it was just an oversight——'

'Good gad!'

'So – so, that's why I – er – well, that's why I came.'

'You came?' repeated the Colonel, as if he couldn't believe his ears. 'You came even though Harry had not invited you?'

'But – but – I knew it was a mistake – wouldn't have overlooked me——'

'Indeed?'

'But when I got here, and they chucked all those beastly snowballs at me, I knew it was only a joke. So that's why I – I just came in quietly. Didn't want to disturb anyone, and that's why I didn't hide in this attic.' He gazed round. 'I must say it's not very comforable. Nearly froze——'

'So you have been hiding up here?'

'No – not hiding. Nothing of the kind. I – I just thought I'd lie doggo for a bit. I – er – um – thought I ought to make sure that Harry really wanted me here, if you see what I mean. He – he said he'd boot me all the way back to Wimford if – if I came. Knew it was really just his little joke. Wouldn't have meant it. Still, I thought I'd just stay doggo – just for a day or two. Make sure——'

The Colonel frowned at Billy Bunter. 'Harry,' he said to his nephew. 'Is this boy in his right mind?'

Harry couldn't help laughing. 'More or less,' he said. 'He can't help being a stupid ass and a blithering idiot.'

'What an extraordinary story,' said Colonel Wharton. 'To come here uninvited, and then to conceal himself in an attic! It's extraordinary, quite extraordinary! I want you to take him to the station in the morning, Harry.'

'Oh, crikey!' squeaked Bunter.

'I want you to make sure that he gets on a train for home.'

'It'll be a pleasure.'

'I'll help,' said Johnny, eagerly.

'We'll all help,' said Frank.

'I – I – I say!' bleated the Owl.

'There is to be no mistake about this,' said the Colonel, sternly. 'I want him off the premises as soon as possible, and you are not to leave him until the train has left.' He shook his head. 'I really cannot imagine what his father will have to say.'

'My – my father!' exclaimed the Owl, in dismay. 'But – but——'

'Of course I shall have to speak to your father. No doubt he is very worried by your absence.'

'No, he ain't,' Bunter said, hastily. 'He – he knows where I am. I left him a note. He knows what chums Harry and——'

'What!' exclaimed Colonel Wharton. 'You led him to believe that Harry had asked you here? I certainly shall have a great deal to discuss when I ring him up.'

'Oh, lor'!' moaned the hapless Owl.

'I've still not finished with you, you stupid boy! What was that about a burglar?'

'But there was one! I saw him. He nearly clobbered me. I – I fought him off – terrible struggle – nearly captured him——'

'Tell us another,' said Johnny.

'But he was here, I tell you! It was the same one. The one who crept up here this afternoon. I frightened him off. He – bolted like a rabbit when he saw me.'

'What's that?' asked the Colonel, sharply.

'I – I frightened him off——'

'There was a villain here this afternoon,' said Wells.

'The one I nearly got,' Bob said.

'That's right,' said the Colonel, thoughtfully. 'Our regular visitor.'

He turned back to Billy Bunter. 'And you are saying that the same man returned this evening.'

'I told you. He went like the wind down those stairs – came back tonight – saw him with my own eyes. He – he got in through this window——'

'Nonsense! Nobody could reach that window. You must have been dreaming, boy.'

'But I didn't!' shrieked Bunter. 'I didn't. He must have got away the same way that he got in. Look, the window's wide open.'

121

'Rubbish! It's true that a thief did escape that way, but no one could hope to climb up.'

'But he did!'

'Balderdash! You frightened yourself. You really are hopeless. You've disturbed the whole house. I've a good mind to box your ears, but no doubt your father will do it for me.'

Billy Bunter was almost speechless with fury. Here he was, telling the truth for once in his life, but no one believed him. 'But he was here! He climbed in——'

'Nonsense!'

'He – he didn't see me straight away. I watched him all the time. He went to the door, and then he pulled up the carpet——'

'He did what?' said the Colonel, bewildered. 'Did you say you saw him pull up the carpet?'

'Yes, and then——'

The Colonel spoke to Wells. 'I think this boy should be seen by a doctor. First of all he wants us to believe that there was a burglar, and now he insists that he was stealing a worthless carpet.'

'I don't want a doctor!' hooted Bunter. 'I – I'm telling the truth. He pulled up the carpet——'

'Now that will do, Bunter. You were dreaming.'

'But he did!' shouted the Owl. 'He did!'

'Be quiet! I don't want to hear any more!'

'I tell you –' yelled Bunter.

'Shut up, old fat man,' said Bob Cherry. 'You've been in the land of nod as usual. What on earth would a burglar want a carpet for?'

'He didn't!'

'Eh?'

'He didn't!' shrieked the Owl. 'He wanted the picture.'

'What?' Bob shot Billy Bunter a puzzled glance.

'He's pottier than ever,' said Frank.

'I'm not potty!'

The Colonel joined Tom Wells. 'The boy is rambling,' he said, quietly. 'Perhaps you can arrange for the doctor to come before he is sent home. I should like to make sure that he is fit to travel.' He turned back to Bunter, and spoke to him in a slightly kindlier tone. 'Now, Bunter, my boy, you can see for yourself that there are no pictures in this attic, and since there are no pictures, I doubt whether there was a burglar.'

'Not on the walls!' gasped Billy Bunter. 'Under the carpet!'

'Good gad! This is more serious than I thought! Now he fancies that pictures are hung under carpets. Late as it is, Wells, I think we had better get in touch with the doctor.'

'The picture's under the carpet!' bellowed Bunter. 'That's what the burglar wanted – the picture, not the carpet!'

'Take it easy, fathead,' murmured Harry Wharton.

'You'll get over it,' Bob assured him.

'There have been tremendous advances in medical science,' said Hurree Singh, soothingly. 'You won't be locked up for long.'

'We'll come and see you,' added Johnny Bull.

'But——'

'Now, now, my boy. All you need is a little rest——'

'I don't! I know what I saw. I saw the burglar——'

'It is becoming an obsession,' said the Colonel, sounding worried. 'My dear boy, you imagined——'

'But I didn't imagine anything!' yelled Bunter, 'Look for yourself!' He stopped, grasped one edge of the old carpet, and threw it back.

There was a long, low whistle from Bob and they all stood, looking in amazement at the large painted canvas – the canvas that glowed with rich, warm colours.

Colonel Wharton stood transfixed. 'The Tintoretto!' he exclaimed.

Billy Bunter blinked around the ring of astounded faces. 'What? I thought it was a picture.' He bent over it. 'It is a picture,' he said, indignantly. 'Anyone can see it's a picture.'

'The Tintoretto,' said the Colonel, again. 'So it wasn't stolen after all. He didn't get away with it. He left it here, and returned for it. Good gad!'

He stooped, and lifted it, with careful hands. That picture was his most prized possession, not because it was worth a vast amount of money, but because he loved it. He always had. Its loss had been a tremendous blow, and now, here it was, safe in his hands again.

'See, I told you so,' said Bunter. 'Now perhaps you'll believe me. I told you there was a burglar, didn't I? He jolly well knew there was a picture under that carpet. I don't know how he knew it was there, but he jolly well did. He went straight to it. It must be worth pounds or he wouldn't have shinned up that drain pipe, would he?'

'Pounds!' said Frank. 'You're a bit out, fat man. It's worth thousands and thousands – a fortune.'

Billy Bunter was startled. 'No!' he said. 'Oh, crikey! No wonder he was after it. How did he know it was there?'

'He knew it was there, my dear Bunter, because he had put it there.'

'Gosh, he must have moved fast that night,' said Harry. 'He must have shoved it under the carpet——'

'Told you so,' said the fat Owl, smugly.

'Barricaded the door and slipped down the drain pipe.'

'We ought to have thought,' said Wells. 'If he'd thrown it down, he'd have damaged it, so he had to put it somewhere. He must have needed both hands to get down the pipe.'

Colonel Wharton looked up from his close inspection of the picture. 'He was so athletic, that it didn't occur to us. To think it was——'

'Under that carpet,' said Harry.

'Well, well, well!' grinned Bob Cherry. 'So Bunter hasn't gone completely round the twist after all. He did see a burglar.'

'Didn't I say so?' hooted the Owl. 'Didn't I tell you he came through that window——'

'A remarkable exploit,' said Hurree Singh, peering out of the window.

'I jolly well saw him——'

'And you jolly well yelled your head off,' said Johnny Bull.

'Fancy old Bunter being right for once,' remarked Bob.

'Oh, really, Cherry!'

'Good gad! That's quite right,' exclaimed the Colonel. 'If this utterly stupid boy had not been here, we should never have found my picture again.'

'Yes, it was a bit of luck,' said Harry.

Billy Bunter beamed. He saw a ray of hope. Although it had

'. . . knew it was there because he had put it there.'

been unintentional, he had been in the right place at the right time. But for him, the Tintoretto would have disappeared for ever. He saw his chance.

'I say, you fellows, I bet you're glad I came.'

'You fat frump!' said Harry.

'What's that?' His face fell. It wasn't the response he had hoped for.

'You're a pernicious porker!'

'No, no – what do you mean, Harry, old chap?'

'But they can be useful sometimes.' Harry laughed at Bunter's puzzled expression. 'What I'm saying, fat man, is that it was lucky you were here.'

'Are you?' Billy Bunter's hopes began to rise again.

'Just for once – yes.'

'Harry,' said Colonel Wharton. 'There is no doubt about it. This ridiculous boy has rendered me a very great service. I know that it was only by chance, but I do have reason to be grateful to him. I have my picture back.' The Bunter beam spread from ear to ear. 'His behaviour has been extraordinary – extraordinary, irresponsible, and incredibly stupid——'

'Oh, I say!' protested Bunter.

'But he did it because he wanted to be with you for Christmas. If that is what he still wants, then I rather feel that we should make him welcome, Harry.'

'Righto!' Harry looked at the Owl. 'Would you like to stay for Christmas?'

Billy Bunter grinned. 'Well, if you make a point of it, old man.'

'But I don't!'

'Hee, hee, hee! You never stop joking, do you, Harry, old chap.'

'Okay, Bunter. Stay,' said Harry.

'Now, Harry,' said the Colonel. 'I must ring Inspector Slade and tell him what has happened. Put Bunter in the room at the far end of the corridor.

'I – I – I say,' squeaked Bunter.

'What is it?' asked the Colonel.

'Can – can I have some supper?'

'Eh?'

Billy Bunter looked pathetic. 'I – I'm awfully hungry – starving. I haven't had anything to eat today except a cake –' Wells shot a dark look at him. 'And some biscuits——' Tom Wells's face became even blacker, but he said nothing. After all, they had got the Tintoretto back. 'And so I'm famished,' Bunter went on. 'I – I never had a chance of getting at the larder and——'

'What was that?'

'I mean – I mean that I – I wasn't going to go there. Wouldn't have been the thing to do. That's why I was sitting up, not waiting to go down to the kitchen, and – and I say, I'm ever so hungry.'

'Very well. Tom, will you see that this – this absurd boy has something to eat?' and the Colonel went downstairs, his precious picture in his hands.

Soon after that the Famous Five went to bed. It had been quite an eventful day, and they were tired. Billy Bunter was tired too, but not too tired to eat and so, as they drifted off to sleep, Bunter busily chewed and chomped until even his capacious stomach could accept no more. And so, when he finally rolled into a comfortable bed and closed his eyes, he too soon fell asleep. Within seconds his snores echoed up and down the corridor, and nothing and no one – not even a couple of dozen burglars – could have awoken him from that deep, deep sleep.

CHAPTER 26
Hauled Before the Inspector

'Snore! Sn-ore! Ssssnore!'

'Hallo, hallo, hallo!' shouted Bob Cherry, but Bunter rumbled on.

'Wake up, Bunter!' said Frank, loudly, but there was no response.

127

'I think I know how to rouse him,' said Hurree. He spoke into Bunter's fat ear. 'Bunter, my friend, a postal order has come for you.'

'Ha, ha, ha!'

Bunter's eyelids didn't open, and his expression didn't change. He just kept on snoring.

'It's no good,' said Harry. 'Even an earthquake wouldn't do it.'

'Lazy frowster!' snorted Johnny.

It was ten o'clock in the morning, and it was a bright, fine day. Sunshine streamed down on to the fast thawing snow, and it glimmered in at the window of Billy Bunter's bedroom so that a beam of light danced on his fat face.

The Famous Five were gathered around him, not because they wanted to, but because they had been asked to wake him up. They would have been far happier to be on the ice for what might have been the last skating session of the holidays. In fact, they'd have been happier still if he hadn't been there at all, but he was, and so they had to make the most of it. They weren't at all keen on their job, but Bunter had a visitor, and so he had to be roused.

It was never easy to wake him up, but hunger usually helped. Today, the alarm clock in his stomach was silent, still content with the food that had been shovelled into it the night before.

'Bunter!' roared Bob. 'Bunter! Bunty! Bunt!' There was another resonant snore.

'Someone wants to see you!' shouted Frank.

'I can do better than that.' Bob leaned over the bed, closed a thumb and finger on Bunter's little blob of a nose, and gave it a jerk.

'Urrrgh! Groooh! Wurrgh! Grrugg!' Bunter opened his eyes. 'Grrh! Led do by doze! Whad's zat? Led do by doze.'

Bob released it. 'There you are. I knew that would do it.'

'Ha, ha, ha!'

'Beast!' Billy Bunter's small round eyes glared indignantly at the faces grinning down on him. 'Lemme alone. Tain't rising bell yet.' There was another burst of laughter, and Bunter frowned. 'Oh!' he suddenly remembered where he was. 'I say, go away. Lemme sleep.'

'Time to get up, fat man.'

'What are you doing here anyway? Tain't right, barging into a fellows room. Haven't finished sleeping yet. It ain't time to get up.'

'Not time to get up! It's ten o'clock,' said Frank.

'That's what I said, tain't time to get up.'

'You lazy lump!' growled Johnny Bull.

'I don't care if it's twelve. Lemme alone. Push off.'

'Come on, fat man,' urged Harry. 'Show a leg.'

'I shall close my eyes,' said Hurree Singh. 'It won't be a pretty sight.'

'Beast!'

'Come on! Get up!'

'Shan't!'

'But look here——'

Billy Bunter looked stubborn. 'I'm not getting up yet. Hop off and tell Wells I'll have brekker in bed at eleven. Now get out and let me sleep.'

'But Bunter, my friend——'

'Shut up! Clear off!'

'You're wanted, you fat ass!' hooted Johnny Bull.

'Stop yelling in my ear, Bull. You've spoiled my dream – ruined it.'

'What was it?' asked Frank, curiously.

'About a Christmas pud!' There was a gale of laughter. 'Can't you stop that row? You're just a lot of oafs. We don't treat our guests like that at Bunter Court. Wouldn't dream of it. Now shut up, and go away,' and Billy Bunter closed his eyes again.

'You really are wanted,' said Harry.

'Don't care!'

'It's Inspector Slade from the Wimford police station——'

'He can take a running jump!'

'He wants to have a talk with you about last night.'

'Tell him to wait.'

'You stupid, puffed-up porker. He can't waste his time hanging about for you.'

'Then he'll have to come back.'

'Come on! Get up!'

Billy Bunter kept his eyes closely shut. He wanted that sleep, and he was jolly well going to get it. Inspector Slade had called, had he? So what? Anyway, what a stupid time to call. Didn't he realize that a chap had to get his shut-eye? No, he could do what he liked – hang about, or go away and come back later, but he wasn't going to have the honour of the Owl's company just yet.

'Why don't we tip him out?' asked Johnny Bull.

Harry shook his head. It was what he would have liked to have done, and it was what he would have done if they had been at Greyfriars. By now he would have been rolled on to the floor in a tangle of bedclothes, but he wasn't at Greyfriars. He was in Wharton Lodge, and he was a guest. Strong-arm methods were out.

He tried again. 'Come on, Bunter. Move your fat carcass.'

'I told you to shut up, Wharton.'

'I can't tell Inspector Slade that you won't get up.'

'Tell him to eat coke then.'

Harry heaved a sigh. 'You know I can't do that either. Just——'

'Shan't!'

'Listen! My uncle will come if you don't appear.'

'You'd better not let that stuffy old stick come barging in here.'

'You – you disgusting worm!'

'That's a fine thing!' said the fat Owl, indignantly. 'Calling a fellow names when you've asked him for Christmas. I thought you'd got better manners than that, Wharton! Now clear off, the lot of you.'

The juniors gave each other exasperated glances, and then Bob gave them a quick wink.

'Oh!' he shouted, in alarm. 'Look out! He's under the bed! Oh, my hat!'

Bunter's eyes flickered open. 'What? What's that?'

'Get out! It's the chap from the attic!' yelled Bob.

'I – I – I say – what?'

'Get out! Run for it, now!'

'What's that in his hand! Quick!'

The Famous Five stampeded to the door, uttering wild cries as they went.

There was a panic-stricken yell from the Owl as he scrambled wildly out of bed.

'Help! Wait for me! Keep him off! Help! Burglars!' As he flung himself from the bed, Bunter's foot became entangled in a trailing blanket, and he rolled over on to the ground. 'Yaroooo! Help! He's got me!' Somehow, he managed to kick himself free, and rushed frantically across the room, hurtled through the door, and pelted headlong into the corridor. Five fellows standing on the other side of the open door chuckled as the fat figure, dressed in an old nightshirt, raced along the passage, making for the stairs.

'He's got up!' said Bob, simply.

'Ha, ha, ha!'

Billy Bunter neither saw nor heard them. He charged on to the landing. There was a thud as he crashed into Colonel Wharton. As the Colonel staggered against the wall, Billy Bunter tottered into his arms.

'Good gad!'

'Ooogh!' gurgled the Owl.

Colonel Wharton pulled himself together and pushed him away. 'You utterly absurd boy!' he exclaimed. 'Why are you rushing about like that?'

'Urrrgh! There's a bub – bub——'

'What?'

'A bub – bub – bib – bib – burglar,' stuttered Bunter. 'There's a bib – bob – burglar under the bob – bub – bed in my room——'

'Goodness gracious!' The Colonel looked at Harry who had followed Bunter along the corridor. 'What does this mean . . . ? Bunter, return to your room immediately and dress yourself, and when you are clean and tidy come downstairs. The inspector is waiting to see you.'

Billy Bunter trembled violently. 'There's a bib – bub – bob——'

'Nonsense!'

'I tell you there's a bib – bob – bub – Ow! Leggo!'

Colonel Wharton did not let go of the fat Owl. He kept his hand firmly clasped on a fat shoulder, and marched him back to his room. The fat Owl looked suspiciously at five grinning faces as he went, and then it dawned on him that they had fooled him.

'Beasts!' he hooted. There was a loud burst of laughter. 'Pulling a fellow's leg like that! Tain't fair!'

'Ha, ha, ha!'

'You had me on.'

'Well done, fatty!' said Bob.

'Beast! Yah!'

The Colonel pushed him into his bedroom 'If you are not out here within ten minutes, I shall come and get you,' he said, sternly.

'Oh, crikey!' groaned the Owl.

'And what is more, unless you are clean, I shall order Wells to take a scrubbing brush to you.'

'Oh, lor'!' moaned Bunter.

'And until you have seen Inspector Slade, there will be no breakfast for you.'

'Golly!' Having to wait for breakfast until after his interview was over wasn't good news, but the knowledge that it would be waiting for him gave him some consolation.

CHAPTER 27

Bunter Knows Best

'I say, you fellows!'

'Goodnight, Bunter!'

'But I say——'

'Roll off to bed, barrel.'

'Listen to me!' hooted the Owl.

'Must we?' groaned Johnny.

The juniors were on their way upstairs. Five of them had spent most of their time having a strenuous time in the fresh air, and were ready for bed. The sixth had had a strenuous time too. He had found that moving from the dining table to an armchair and back again was pretty exhausting, but he wasn't thinking of sleep. He was standing at the top of the stairs on the balcony, blinking along the corridor that led to the attic stairs, and looking very uneasy.

'What's the trouble?' asked Harry.

'That man,' said Bunter, nervously.

'What man?'

'Oh, really Wharton! You know. Him. Suppose he came back? Mind you, I'm not afraid. I don't want you thinking that.'

'Of course you aren't. You weren't afraid of him last night. You just happened to be shaking like a jelly,' said Bob.

'Ha, ha, ha!'

As they roared, Billy Bunter looked indignantly at them. 'That's right. Cackle away, but if he came back, you'd be jolly thankful that I'm around.'

'You bet,' said Frank, keeping a straight face.

'But – but still, he's not likely to, is he?'

'Not a hope,' said Harry. 'Not a chance in a million. He must know that the game's up here. I expect he'll be at the other end of the country by now.'

'But all the same——'

'Even if he is still round here, what can he do? All the doors and windows are locked and bolted——'

'But what about the attic window?' squeaked Bunter. 'He got up there once. He could do it again.'

Harry laughed. 'Then he'd have to get down again. It's screwed up on the inside now. That window's so tightly fixed that even a fly couldn't get in. Now, do roll off——'

Bunter gave a nervous twitch. 'He might get down the chimney.'

'And so might Father Christmas,' said Bob.

'Beast!'

'Bed, Bunter, my friend,' said Hurree. 'Let Bob be the beast while you concentrate on being the sleeping beauty.'

'Ha, ha, ha!'

'You can laugh,' said the Owl, 'but I'm jolly well telling you that I'm not going to bed to be burgled. I'm going up to the attic to make sure before I turn in. You know he can climb like a cat. You've heard of cat burglars, haven't you? And he's after

133

that picture——'

'That picture's safe and sound, and hanging in the library, and that's where it's going to stay. Don't worry. It's all under control.'

'I've had enough,' announced Johnny. 'I'm going to bed.'

'I'm not surprised. Trust you to clear off when there might be danger,' jeered the Owl. 'You'll feel a fool in the morning when you wake up and find the picture's gone.'

'Fathead!'

'Idiot!'

'Scared to come up, are you? Well, I'll go on my own. I'm not afraid to tackle him. I'll knock him into a cocked hat.' He eyed the Famous Five anxiously. 'But I wouldn't like to do you out of the chance of showing him what's what.'

'Wouldn't you?'

'No. I don't want all the glory.'

'Oh come on,' said Bob, impatiently. 'If we don't go, we'll have him yammering on all night. Get your torch, Harry, and let's search that rotten old attic. At least it'll shut him up.'

'Right.' Harry sped off and soon came back with the torch, and the procession set off with the uneasy Owl in the rear.

The Famous Five thought it a waste of time. Even if the burglar was still in the neighbourhood, he didn't have a chance of getting into the house. All that he'd be able to catch would be a cold.

Bob paused at the foot of the stairs. 'Hold on,' he said. 'This isn't right. It's Bunter's show, not ours.'

'Quite right,' said Frank, promptly. 'We can't steal his thunder. Come on, fatty. Take your place at the head of your troops.'

'I – I've got to tie my shoelace. You fellows get on. I'll catch you up.'

'That's all right. We'll wait.'

'No. It's – it's got into a bit of a knot.'

As they burst into laughter, Harry said, 'I've got a feeling that it'll take him some time to tie that shoelace. Let's move.'

Harry led the way upstairs, and pushed open the attic door. The five of them trampled around while Bunter blinked from the doorway, but as they had expected, the room was empty.

Bunter glinted towards the small window. 'Sure that's safe?'

Harry flashed the light on to it. 'It's as safe as houses. It's got about a dozen screws in it.'

'No one could get in there,' said Bob. 'Anything else, fat man?'

'Wh – what about the chimney?' he asked.

'Dope!'

'But he could have climbed on the roof——'

'Or he might have sprouted wings and flown up there,' suggested Hurree.

'Don't be daft!' snapped Bunter. 'He could have climbed up the chimney and – well, you could see if anyone could get down it.'

'Ass!'

'Fathead!'

'Nitwit!'

'Oh, we might as well,' said Harry, with an air of resignation. 'Then we can go to bed.'

He stooped down. 'Gosh! It's a socking great chimney,' he said, and directed a beam of light up it, 'but –' his voice died away. There, dangling just above his head, was a foot!

Harry's eyes nearly popped out of his head. Where there was a foot, there had to be a leg, and that leg had to be attached to a body – a body that was coming down the chimney. Bunter had been right!

There was a chuckle from behind. 'Anybody, there, old bean?'

'If there is, yank him down.'

'See if he's got a red coat and a hood and a long, white beard.'

'Ha, ha, ha!'

Their laughter jerked Harry into action. He held the torch in his left hand, reached up with his right, grabbed an ankle, and pulled.

'Aaaagh!' There was a startled yell.

'What's that?'

'Who——?'

'Oh, my hat!'

As Harry tugged again, there was the sound of something

*A body, covered in soot, crashed down into the grate, and then
rolled on to the floor.*

slithering and down came a leg.

'Quick!'

They grabbed the leg, and pulled. A body, covered in soot, crashed down into the grate, and then rolled on to the floor.

There was a yell from Billy Bunter. 'It's him!'

'Old rat-eyes,' roared Bob. 'Collar him!' Bob was right. It was the rat-eyed burglar. Sprawling and spluttering he made an effort to get to his feet, but he didn't have a chance. The Famous Five piled on top of him. Bob and Johnny grabbed his arms while Frank and Hurree seized his legs, and Harry grasped at his collar. In fact, there were so many hands clutching at him that it seemed there wasn't enough of that thin body to go round.

Billy Bunter didn't go into action, but he made up for it as he babbled and burbled in a state of wild excitement.

'It's him! It's jolly well him! It's him again! I say, you fellows, hold tight – don't let him slip away. I say, watch out. Hang on.'

'It's all right. We've got him!' gasped Bob.

'He won't get away, my dear Bunter!' panted Hurree Singh.

'He doesn't stand a chance!' said Johnny, grimly.

'Now we've got him, we're not letting him go,' said Harry. 'Gosh! What a surprise for Uncle James!'

Unexpectedly, the man stopped struggling. He realized that the game was up. There was nothing he could do against five fit fellows. He shot black looks of hatred at them, but said nothing.

'I say, you fellows!' The fat Owl was almost bouncing up and down in his excitement. 'I told you so, didn't I? I said he'd come back.'

'That's right, fat man,' admitted Harry.

'I said he'd come down the chimney.'

'Right again.'

'If I hadn't said so——'

Bob nodded. 'If you hadn't been a great, fat, nervous nitwit——'

'And a terrified twit,' added Johnny.

'Oh, really, Cherry! That's a bit much, Bull!'

'But it's true,' Bob went on. 'If Bunter hadn't been in such a blue funk, we'd all have gone to bed, and this rat-faced tick would have been able to stroll downstairs, collect the booty, and stroll off again.'

'Mm,' agreed Harry. 'It was a bit of luck that Bunter was scared out of his wits——'

'Not that he has many to be scared out of.'

'Yah!' snorted Billy Bunter. 'You'd have been a fat lot of good without me. He'd have pinched that picture again while you were snoring away. It was me that thought of it. Me that thought of the chimney. You wouldn't have been any good without me.'

'All right. Now shut up about it. Let's cart our prisoner downstairs and hand him over,' said Bob.

'What do you mean – your prisoner!' said the Owl, indignantly. 'Mine, not yours. It was me what done it. Me.'

'Fine,' said Bob. 'He's all yours.'

'Hand him over,' said Frank.

'That's right. Help yourself, Bunter,' Johnny grinned.

Billy Bunter, a look of terror on his face, backed out of the attic. 'I – I – I say, you fellows –' he stammered.

'But he's got to have the glory,' insisted Bob. 'Come on, fat man. Grab him.'

'I – I – I say. I – I – I think you'd better hang on to him,' gasped Bunter. 'I – I'll larry the kite – I mean, I'll carry the light. Can't risk dropping it. I'll take charge of it since you're a clumsy lot of clowns.'

Harry Wharton laughed. 'Come on,' he said.

They marched the rat-eyed man out of the attic, down the stairs, along the corridor and into the hall where Colonel Wharton was sitting by the fireside, smoking a cigar. He lifted his head at the trampling of feet, stared at the extraordinary procession coming towards him, and then jumped up from his chair.

For a moment he was speechless. 'What – what – what?' he stuttered. 'Who – who –? What –?'

'We've nabbed him! It's the thief,' said Bob.

'The thief! Good gad!' He stared at the scowling face.

'He was in the attic!'

'Up the chimney!'

138

'Thought he'd pay us another little visit.'

'Good gad!' said the Colonel again. 'The attic! But – but – why – whatever were you doing there?'

'Bunter got himself into a sweat,' explained Bob. 'He thought that this tick might come down the chimney——'

'Down the chimney?'

'And that's what he was doing. He dropped into our hands like a ripe apple.'

Colonel Wharton rang the bell. 'Harry. Go and ring Inspector Slade. We must give him in charge straight away. Good gad! And it was Bunter, that absurd boy Bunter – Goodness gracious!'

'It was me all the time,' said Bunter, happily. 'Me. If it hadn't been for me, they'd have been asleep. I made them go into the attic. It was me who thought——'

'Yes, Colonel Wharton,' said Wells, coming into the hall, and then he stopped, his eyes fixed on the burglar. 'It's you!' he exclaimed.

'Yes. Harry is telephoning Inspector Slade. We'll lock him up until the police arrive.'

'Well, that's that,' said the Colonel, a note of satisfaction in his voice, once their prisoner had been taken away.

'I done it,' boasted the Owl. 'It was me, me all the time.'

Colonel Wharton turned a kindly eye on him. 'Indeed,' he said. 'It was you all the time.'

'Lucky I came for Christmas,' said the Owl, complacently.

CHAPTER 28

A Merry Christmas!

'Ooooh!' wailed Billy Bunter.

'Hallo, hallo, hallo!'

'Ooooooh!'

'What's the matter?'

'Wooooooh!'

They had had lunch early on Christmas day, but lunch could never be too early for Bunter. When they sat down at the table, he had beamed at the sight of the laden table.

As he had packed away helping after helping, Colonel and Mrs Wharton had cast anxious glances at him, but the Famous Five, used to the Bunter appetite, had hardly noticed. But at last he had finished eating and had left the table, still gazing wistfully at the food that he hadn't been able to polish off, and he had rolled away.

He hadn't rolled far. He had rolled into the hall, and he had collapsed into an armchair by the fire, and he had gazed with glassy eyes at the bright flames. Even he wondered if he had overdone it.

Now, a little later, he was clasping his fat paws over his stomach, and he was groaning. The Famous Five gathered round.

'Enjoying life?' Bob Cherry asked.

'Oooooh!'

'Something wrong?' asked Frank.

'Woooooh!'

'Feeling ill?' asked Harrt Wharton.

'Nunno! I – I'm all right. I – I just feel a little queer, that's all. Can't think why.'

'Neither can I,' said Johnny Bull. 'It isn't as if you ate very much.'

'Not more that an elephant needs,' said Hurree Singh.

'Couldn't have been the turkey. Wasn't that. I only had four helpings.'

'Then it wasn't that,' agreed Bob.

'Wasn't the Christmas pud either. Only had seven of those.'

'It couldn't have been that then.'

'And it wasn't anything to do with the mince pies. Why, I didn't help myself to more than a dozen or so.'

'Perhaps it was the whole lot put together,' suggested Bob, and they burst into laughter.

'Ooooh!' moaned Bunter. 'Wooooh! I say, you fellows – oooh! Wooooh! I – I don't feel well, really I don't. Ooooh! Can't you stop cackling? Don't know what you're laughing about. Oooooh!'

Although the Famous Five were sympathetic, there wasn't much they could do for a fat Owl within whose extensive circumference four helpings of turkey were on bad terms with seven of Christmas pud, and all of them at war with a dozen or more mince pies, and so they went out into the open air, leaving Bunter to recover at his leisure.

When, an hour or two later, they came in, Billy Bunter was still sitting in the same armchair by the blazing fire, but it was a different Billy Bunter. A brighter, bouncier fat Owl blinked at them through his big, round specs. 'I say, you fellows!' he squawked.

'Hallo, hallo, hallo!'

'I say, is it tea time?'

The Famous Five roared with laughter. Evidently, Bunter had recovered.